Fat Louise

JAMIE BEGLEY

Fat Louise

Young Ink Press Publication
YoungInkPress.com

Copyright © 2015 by Jamie Begley
Edited by C&D Editing, and Hot Tree Editing
Cover Art by Young Ink Press

ISBN-13: 978-0692412275
ISBN-10: 0692412271

Prologue

Benedict Montgomery stepped inside the dirty bar, trying not to show his fear as the few people inside all turned to look at him in the doorway.

The Corpus Christi heat outside was stifling, and it wasn't much cooler inside the dim bar.

Tugging at his shirt collar, he walked past the tables to the bar as the Mexican bartender raised the bar's divider, coming to stand in front of him.

"I'm looking for Cade Reed."

"What do you want to drink?" the bartender asked, moving back behind the bar, making it obvious he wasn't there to give out information for free.

"A beer will be fine."

Once a beer was set down in front of him, Benedict laid some money down on the counter. When the bartender remained silent, he added several more bills to the pile.

"He's out back. It won't take long. Have a seat." He moved away to wait on someone at the end of the bar.

Benedict took a table at the side of the bar where he self-consciously sipped on his beer while he waited.

Moments later, a door on the other side of the bar opened, and a tall man appeared with his arm around a pretty Mexican woman. They took a seat at one of the tables against the wall, obscuring them in shadows.

The bartender nodded his head in their direction, letting Benedict know that was the man he was looking for.

Benedict rose from his table, trying to talk himself out of leaving. Only the desperation he felt made him cross the bar to face the man sitting in the shadows.

He had to clear his throat before he could get the name out. "Cade Reed?"

Dark eyes studied him impassively. "Who's asking?"

"I'm Benedict Montgomery. I'd like to talk to you privately, if I may?"

"Why?"

"I would like to offer you a job."

"I'm retired. Leave before one of the locals decide to take that wad of cash in your pocket. I'm not interested." With that, he started to nuzzle the neck of the woman he had come in with. Her sensuous whispers made it obvious the couple had a sexual relationship, something he and his wife hadn't shared in far longer than Benedict cared to think about. It had been a long time since his wife and he had even talked cordially to each other, much less communicated as lovers.

Benedict could understand Cade not wanting to leave the beautiful woman running her hands over his chest.

"George Connell sent me."

An aggravated sigh came from Cade before he lifted his head and stared at Benedict balefully. With a nod toward the bar, he said, "Martina, give me ten minutes."

"That's all it ever takes you," she giggled, standing up, and Cade spanked her retreating ass for the comment.

Once she left, Benedict took a chair across the table from the man who didn't look like he was happy with the interruption.

"What do you want?"

"George gave me your name. He said you could get my daughters back for me."

Cade raised a sardonic brow. "Exactly where are your daughters?"

"Peñuela. It's a city in the south of Mexico."

"I know where the fuck it is, and the answer is no. Tell George to find someone else who wants to die. It's a suicide mission."

Benedict went pale at his response. "There is no one else. Connell only gave me your name because I wouldn't leave him alone."

"Then you're shit out of luck." He motioned for Martina to come back.

"Please. I'll pay you anything you want. I'm a rich man. I would go in after them myself, but I'm prohibited from going to Peñuela because I occasionally work for the Government."

Cade waved the woman away again, and Benedict paused, taking a deep breath.

"How much money are we talking?"

Benedict licked his dry lips, taking a drink of his beer before asking, "What would it take?"

"I don't know. Let me think. It's dangerous. Hell, a dead man can't spend money, no matter how much it is, but there is a number that would make me willing to take the chance…"

"What is it?"

"A hundred grand."

"Okay," Benedict answered immediately.

Cade's eyes narrowed on him. "I'm thinking I should have asked for more."

Benedict set his beer down on the dirty table. "If you get my daughters out, I'll give you an extra hundred as a bonus."

"We're talking about U.S. dollars, right?"

Benedict nodded.

"Damn, that's hard to turn down. One woman may be possible to get out, but two is going to be close to hopeless," he mused to himself. "I'll be dodging the gangs and the Federales. A man disappears down there in the blink of an eye."

"I'll make it three hundred. A hundred for each of my girls. Plus another hundred thousand dollar bonus when I have them back."

"Fuck me." Cade whistled under his breath. "You have a deal."

Benedict sat back in his chair, shaking. He reached into his pocket, pulled out a handkerchief, and wiped his forehead. He would have paid twice that to have his daughters back.

"I didn't know anyone still used those things."

Benedict blushed, hastily putting the handkerchief back in his pocket before going to another pocket to pull out two photographs, laying them on the table between them.

"The one on the right is my youngest daughter, Bailey, the other is Jane. Jane's blond in the picture but she dyed her brown hair a few days before she disappeared. I should have realized then what she had planned."

"They aren't going to want to give Bailey up easily," Cade remarked.

"She married a young man from Mexico while she was in college her freshman year." Benedict gave a twisted smile. "I begged her to wait, but she wouldn't listen. They went to Puebla to visit some of her husband's relatives. That was when Marcus lured her into going into Peñuela." Benedict shook his head at his daughter's innocence.

He had begged her not to go there, telling her about the travel warnings in place, but again, she had refused to listen, placing all her faith in her new husband.

"When we didn't hear from Bailey, we became worried." He swallowed hard. "It took some investigating before we found out Marcus's family is heavily involved with a drug cartel and wouldn't allow her to leave. My wife and I were searching for a way to get her back when my other daughter, Jane, went in after her. She's now also disappeared."

Both men stared down at the picture of Jane, who was the opposite of Bailey. Bailey was tall and blond with rounded feminine curves, which were fully displayed in the little black dress she was wearing. Her golden skin showed she either spent hours lazing in the sun or in a tanning bed. From the spoiled tilt of her sensuous lips, Cade was willing to bet it was the former. She was smiling in the picture, basking in the attention of whoever was holding the camera. Cade would bet his last large paycheck that the glamorous blond acted like an entitled bitch.

Cade shifted his attention back to the next picture. Jane was thin, and everything about her screamed nondescript. She faded into the background of the ugly couch she was curled up on. There was nothing that would make her stand out; therefore, she wouldn't pose any of the problems her more attractive sister would in getting her out. There were only two things that made him take a second look—the silvery tint to her eyes and plump lips that had his dick taking notice. After fucking Martina, he wouldn't have thought it was possible to be turned on by a pair of lips.

"That one will be easier to get out." Cade tapped the photograph of Jane.

Benedict stiffened at the unintentional insult yet kept his mouth closed.

"The last time I went in, I retrieved a young man who had gone down to find himself; instead, his ass was kidnapped. He was a rich kid who felt guilty being born into a wealthy family and thought he would make the world a better place for those less fortunate. He was lucky to get out alive. I made several enemies getting him out. I don't suppose Bailey's husband would be willing to come back? It would make it much easier with his help."

Benedict shook his head. "He threatened to kill Bailey if she tried to leave him."

Cade's finger tapped Jane's picture. "Why did she go in? She had to have known how dangerous it would be. Did she want to find a man for herself? She wouldn't be the first woman to romanticize…"

Benedict sadly shook his head. "That's not the case with Jane. My wife egged her on, telling her she should do more to help." His hands tightened on the now empty beer bottle. "She was trying to get Bailey back."

Cade's mouth curled. "Let me guess; she's not her daughter."

"No. I had Jane during my first marriage. Her mother raised her, and I was allowed to spend too little time with her. The aftermath of that was I unfortunately aided my wife in spoiling Bailey to make up for my absence in Jane's life because I was allowed to spend so little time with Jane. However, I recently retired from my business, so I moved closer to Jane with Bailey gone. I stepped down in my role with the government to an advisory capacity to be near her."

Cade laughed, throwing his head back. "Jesus. No matter how screwed up the relationship is, she should have been smarter than to think she could actually succeed in getting her sister out."

"I should have known she would try something. She loves Bailey." Benedict blamed himself, knowing he should have anticipated Jane trying to accomplish what no one else could.

"How long have they been in Mexico?"

"Bailey, two months, and Jane, a week."

"How did Jane hope to find her?"

"I have no idea," he admitted.

"Well, you haven't given me an easy job. I'll get on a flight tomorrow and see what I can do. In the meantime…"—he motioned toward the woman— "Martina, give me a pencil and a piece of paper!"

The woman set the items he wanted down on the table and then brushed her mouth against his before leaving them alone again.

Cade wrote down a series of numbers and the name of a bank on the paper. "I expect a down payment of two hundred thousand in my bank before I board the plane. The rest of the money is to be given to George until I get back."

"I'll see that it gets done," Benedict promised, standing up with the paper in his hand.

"Montgomery?" Cade's voice halted Benedict's departure. "Which one?"

"Which one?" he asked in confusion.

"If I can only get one out alive, which one do you want it to be?" Cade gave a hard sigh yet stared at him pitilessly. "In other words, if I'm in hot water and both are drowning, and I can save only one, which one do you want me to save?"

Benedict felt his heart rip in two at the choice he was being asked to make. No parent ever wanted to make the decision the cold-hearted bastard was asking of him. Staring back at Reed's unforgiving face, he felt his shoulders drop in defeat as he came to a decision he didn't really want to make.

"Bailey. She couldn't make it on her own. Jane's a strong swimmer; she would stand a better chance of surviving." Benedict left the bar with tears clogging his throat, restraining himself from going back inside and changing his answer. Jane was strong—she wouldn't drown—and he was putting his faith in Cade Reed. George had said he was the best mercenary in the business.

He paused, sucking in a deep breath to calm himself.

Jane's image came to mind—her sweet smile and how she was constantly trying to make everyone happy. It wouldn't be as easy as Cade thought to leave his eldest daughter behind.

When he had divorced his first wife, he had thought it would be easy to leave; however, his love for Jane hadn't disappeared or lessened with her absence. Instead, it had grown stronger. He had eventually caved in to his ex-wife's vindictive demands just to spend an occasional weekend with Jane.

Benedict had to tell himself both of his daughters would survive; otherwise, he wouldn't be able to board the plane home to a woman he had long ago stopped caring about.

He'd had Jane when he was eighteen and Bailey when he was twenty-one. He had stuck this marriage out because he wasn't about to lose another daughter to divorce. With Bailey gone, his marriage was fast approaching the end.

The only way he was able to leave was knowing Cade wouldn't have an easy time abandoning Jane.

His mouth quirked in the beginning of a smile. Cade was about to meet a woman hard to resist. In fact, Benedict found a new worry—that he might not be able to get her back from Cade once he realized how special she was.

Chapter One

Jane hid behind one of the large SUVs that had been stolen at a roadblock and was now being used to either transport drugs or young women.

Her mouth tightened into a grim line. The men were nothing but rapists, using the women as sex slaves. They sickened Jane. The thought of her sister being married to one made her want to shake Bailey the minute she managed to find her. As she waited for the bus, her thoughts went back to how she had managed to get herself into a predicament that rivaled the night Sex Piston's beauty shop had been robbed. At least that fiasco had been over in a matter of hours; this hare-brained scheme of hers seemed to be lasting forever.

When Bailey had told them she was going to Peñuela, she had tossed her parents' and Jane's warnings away, as if they hadn't known what they were talking about. Now she

1

was trapped, and Jane had foolishly sneaked in to attempt a rescue.

It hadn't taken her long to regret her impetuous decision to try to save her sister. If she hadn't managed to catch a few lucky breaks, she would have already returned to her small apartment in the safety of the town her father lived in.

About a week before, she entered Mexico and managed to latch on to John and Sandra Terrell, who were trying to get their son back—the son had come down on vacation and never returned. Instead, the parents had received a call demanding a ransom.

John was ex-military and was attempting to go into Mexico to save their son. Jane met them at the hotel where she was staying and joined them during dinner. When they found out why she was going to Mexico, they quickly tried to dissuade her. Seeing that she wasn't going to give up, they attempted to help her by John including her in his plans. It was dangerous, but it just might work. At least it was better than what she had planned—heading straight to Peñuela and demanding to see Bailey.

Sandra remained behind, giving Jane the chance to enter Mexico unnoticed. John and Jane crossed the border with her pretending to be his wife. The guards didn't even blink at the identification she had presented to them after she slipped them a handful of cash to ignore the lack of similarities between her and the picture.

Once across the border, they were staying in the same hotel John's son had used when they were dragged out of their room in the middle of the night. John was taken away in a heavily armed Jeep, while Jane was escorted to a small house that contained several other women.

The three days she was forced to spend there were horrifying. She repeatedly witnessed women being dragged out after men came in and surveyed them.

She was about to lose hope when the door was thrust open, and John appeared in the doorway. She quickly stood, moving toward him and remaining silent as fear screamed through her veins. After she followed John to the same Jeep they had left in three days ago, they climbed in and took off.

Inside the Jeep, a man dressed in military fatigues was driving while another stood in the rear with a rifle. John sat in the front seat next to the driver, and a tanned man she knew to be John's son from the many pictures Sandra had shown her sat next to her.

They were heading back to the border, and while her nerves were relieved to be going home, her anxiety rose as she realized she was leaving her sister behind.

After they left the city, John reached for a canteen of water, handing it to her in the backseat. She took a long drink of the warm water then offered it to John's son, only to receive a shake of his head.

When she reached forward to hand it back to John, he took it and smashed it down on the head of the driver. The Jeep lost control as the driver spun out, trying to hang on to the steering wheel John was attempting to wrench from his control.

Jane clung to the seat in front of her for dear life, terrified she would be thrown out.

As the fighter behind her loosened his hold on the Jeep, bringing his weapon up to fire, Jane saw John's son reach back and push the guard out of the back of the careening vehicle. Just as the yell sounded from the falling man, the driver managed to bring the Jeep to a stop and then fought with John in the front seat. Jane watched as John's son leaned forward, putting the fighter in a chokehold from behind until he stopped moving.

"John!" Jane screamed, seeing the man who had fallen out of the back running toward them.

John reached over to the opposite side of the driver, pulling his weapon free. With one smooth move, he twisted in his seat bringing the pistol up. John aimed to miss his son and fired, several pops came from the pistol,

3

and the fighter fell to the ground.

Everyone sat frozen for several seconds before John and his son jumped from their seats.

"Hurry, Jane. We don't have long." The men pulled the dead driver from his seat, taking off his clothes. Jane couldn't understand what they were doing. "Get your clothes off. I'll stash them in my backpack," John ordered.

The urgency John showed didn't give her time to feel shy about disrobing in front of the men. Taking off her clothes, she threw them aside before pulling the khaki trousers up her hips. They were long on her yet not too bad. Her fingers trembled so badly she barely managed to lace up the boots they threw toward the pile of clothes laying on the ground. Grabbing the large shirt, she quickly buttoned it closed. The last part was the cap, which she clumsily put on.

"Try to hide your face as much as possible," John said, studying her critically.

John's son went to the dead guard lying on the ground next to the one John had shot. He picked up the gun and handed it to Jane along with the canteen.

"Do you know how to shoot?"

"No," she said, holding it cautiously. John took it from her, giving her a series of instructions she knew she wouldn't be able to remember.

"I tried to find out what I could about your sister. As far as I could piece together, you might still be able to find her in Peñuela. This is as far as Matthew and I can go, though. We're getting our asses out of here. Do you want to come with us?" He handed her the backpack he had stuffed her clothes into.

"I have to try," Jane said softly. She was unbelievably scared. She wanted to cling to the safety of the two men, but she couldn't leave without Bailey. If John had been successful, maybe she stood a chance, as well.

"I can't leave the Jeep. Besides, you'll have an easier time passing unnoticed if you try to fit in. Not too many

4

will try to confront you in the clothes you're wearing," John said apologetically.

"I understand."

Matthew climbed into the Jeep. "Dad, we have to go before someone comes along and finds us."

"Good luck." With that, John climbed into the vehicle without a backward glance.

"You, too." The two men didn't hear her response as they took off, leaving her alone in a cloud of dust.

She took buses during the day, ignoring the wary looks others gave her. Finding somewhere to hide that night, her luck held out, and no one recognized her as a woman. The next morning, she put dirt on her face and hands to disguise her features, and thanks to the many hours she had spent in Spanish class, she was able to pass through several cities without trouble. She also found a spot to bury the clothes that would identify her as a woman. If anyone decided to search the backpack she carried, the only thing they would find was an innocuous tube of medicine and some meal replacement bars.

Thankfully, the research to get prepared for finding her sister had clued her in on where to stay away from in her journey to Peñuela. Jane had heard that several areas in Mexico were dangerous, but she had no clue as to just how much until she was sitting at a small restaurant when a gun battle broke out on the sidewalk outside. She dove under her table with her hands over her ears until she heard the gunfire stop. Afterward, she almost lost the lunch she had just eaten when she saw the bodies lying in the street.

Over the next few days, she was on buses that were routinely checked by someone dressed in military garb who would often demand toll fees from everyone onboard before the vehicle was allowed to proceed.

Shaking herself out of her reverie, she saw the bus she had been waiting on slide to a stop. Casually, she walked out from her hiding place and stepped onto the bus, handing the driver the money to cover her fare before taking a seat toward the back.

Jane hunkered down in her seat, trying to go unnoticed on the crowded bus. If she stayed on this particular bus, it would take her to Córdoba. She would stay there until she could find a way to Peñuela.

A young woman on the seat next to her kept giving her curious looks. Usually, others would glance away when she caught them looking at her, but this woman didn't. Jane was startled when she suddenly stood up, sliding into the seat next to her. Jane cast her a startled look, praying she wouldn't start flirting with her. It wouldn't be the first time a young woman had, and Jane had felt uncomfortable rebuffing the women when it happened.

"You have family in Córdoba?"

"No." Jane lowered her voice, trying to sound masculine.

The woman was dark-haired and beautiful. Jane would never be able to compete with her in the beauty department, even when she was dressed as a woman in her tightest leather outfit.

"My name is Carina."

Jane remained quiet, hoping her silence would drive her away. Instead, she began talking about her family in Ciudad Valles before speaking of her own life. "I work in a bar in Córdoba."

Jane wondered frantically why Carina kept divulging so much information about herself. The woman had to be aware of the danger she was putting herself in.

"I deal with men every day. They have certain habits that are hard to hide." Jane stiffened, looking at the woman out of the corner of her eye. "Men do not cross their legs."

Jane hastily uncrossed hers.

"Why are you pretending to be a man?" Jane saw no malice in her face, only curiosity.

"I thought it would be safer," Jane answered quietly, trying to keep her voice lowered so no one else could hear.

"Possibly. On the other hand, it could be even more dangerous if another man wants to challenge you."

"I'd rather take my chances with a gun battle than be kidnapped and raped."

Carina's eyes darkened. "I see you have been listening to all the gossip about Mexico in United Sates."

Jane felt ashamed of herself. She didn't want to assume the worst, but witnessing the captive women and her knowledge of Bailey's confinement had her on her guard.

"I'm sorry."

"Don't be. It is dangerous; however, as long as you're cautious, you will be safe. If you're so concerned for your safety, why are you traveling alone and going to Córdoba?"

Jane decided to be truthful.

"I'm trying to find my sister. She recently came to Mexico to visit her husband's relatives in Peñuela and never returned home."

"Maybe she doesn't want to?" Carina's face had paled when Jane mentioned Peñuela.

Jane shook her head. "Her last text message was to my father, saying her husband wanted them to stay longer, but she wanted to come home."

"You are going to Peñuela?"

"As soon as I can catch the next bus."

"You know where she is in Peñuela?"

"No. I only met her husband once, and we didn't talk much."

"You can't go knocking on people's doors, asking questions," Carina warned.

"I know that. I thought I would ask around if anyone knew Raul's family, Silva." Actually, she had been so focused in trying to reach Peñuela safely that she hadn't given much thought to how she would find where her sister was living.

Carina's face went white. She gripped Jane's arm tightly. "You can't do that!" she hissed.

"Why?"

This time it was Carina's turn to remain silent.

"Please tell me," Jane pleaded.

"I have heard of the Silva family. They are very dangerous and involved in many things I do not want to know about. My cousin worked in the bar before I did. She met someone from the Silva organization, and they became involved." Carina shuddered. "She moved to Peñuela to be with him and rarely sees her family anymore. They keep their women close."

Jane already knew that piece of information. Bailey wouldn't have easily given up her pampered lifestyle in the United States unless she had been forced to.

Jane's mind whirled as she tried to think about what her next step should be.

"Where are you going to stay tonight? No bus will be leaving for Peñuela so late."

"I don't know."

"Stay with me. I think I may have an idea to help."

Jane stared at her steadily, attempting to decide if she should trust the woman.

Carina's tanned complexion was smooth and without blemish, her dark eyes clear and straightforward, and the long mass of black hair had been swept away from her beautiful face. It was ultimately the concern in her expression for a stranger that had Jane deciding to trust her.

"I'll stay the night and take the bus tomorrow. Thanks."

After Carina nodded in response, they talked quietly as the bus drove. Carina told her more about her large family as well as her fiancé who was also waiting for her in Ciudad Valles.

"He doesn't mind you being away?"

"No, we are saving money to buy a home when we get married." Carina took her phone out of her pocket to show a picture of a handsome man standing next to her. It was obvious by way they were staring into each other's eyes that they were very much in love. It was the same expression Jane had caught on Sex Piston's and Stud's faces when they thought themselves unobserved.

It was almost dark when the bus entered Córdoba, but there was enough light for Jane to see the city was much larger than she had envisioned.

She got off the bus and walked next to Carina, trying to keep up with her fast pace.

"I thought you said it wasn't as dangerous as I had heard," Jane puffed.

"It isn't until it gets dark."

Jane gazed up at the rapidly darkening sky. "How much longer?"

"Not far." Carina turned down one street then another, the buildings getting farther and farther apart and older and older as they passed. She made a right onto a street that was almost completely dark, the only light coming from a sign outside a small building.

Carina pointed in relief. "That's it. Come on."

Jane's wariness returned, but she foolishly followed, telling herself everything would be fine. If Killyama were there, she would kick her ass for being so trusting.

Carina didn't go in the front door, going instead to the back where she kicked a beer bottle out of their path that led up a flight of steps. Taking a key from her pocket, she opened the door. Jane took a hesitant step inside, instantly relieved when she saw the bright apartment.

"It's very pretty," Jane complimented, staring at the bright red couch with the small coffee table sitting in front of it. It had a small kitchen with two stools sitting in front of the counter that was tiled in a myriad of bright colors.

"The couch pulls out into a bed. I share the apartment with Teresa. We sleep in the bedroom." She pointed to an open doorway down a small hallway. "She's working downstairs in the bar tonight. I need to get changed and go down to help out. Will you be all right alone?"

"Yes. I'll take a shower if you don't mind and get some

sleep."

"That sounds good. I'll be back after my shift." She went inside the bedroom and closed the door.

Jane found a hiding place for her backpack with the gun inside before taking off her cap. She ran her fingers through her damp hair, feeling its filthiness. Although she was anxious to take a shower and wash the grime away, she wasn't thrilled about having to put her dirty clothes back on.

Carina came out of the bedroom dressed in a loose black skirt and a bright pink T-shirt, packing a bundle of clothes in her hands. "I didn't know if you had anything to sleep in, so I brought you an extra gown of mine." She handed Jane the small gown that she was sure would reach the floor. Carina was much taller than her. "I need to go; I'm already late."

"Go ahead. I'll be fine," Jane assured her, trying to hide her uncertainty.

Carina went to the front door. "If you hear a key in the door, don't be scared. Sometimes, Teresa brings someone upstairs to the bedroom for a little while. I'll tell her to be quiet so she won't wake you."

"Thanks." Jane didn't know what else to say.

Her new friend simply nodded before going out the door, leaving her alone.

Jane stood still for several minutes, merely staring at the closed door, wondering if she had lost her mind to trust someone she had just met. She really didn't have any other options at that point. She would get some sleep then catch the bus to Peñuela in the morning.

She went into the tiny bathroom, taking off her filthy clothes while the bath filled with water before getting in. She laid her head back as she soaked, letting the tension ease out of her shoulders.

She was jerked awake when she heard the front door slam shut and voices coming from the living room. Jane almost slipped and fell out of the tub as she climbed out.

Drying off, she heard them pass the bathroom and go inside the bedroom. She pulled on the nightgown Carina had given her and then left the bathroom to go back to the living room.

The couch was easily pulled out into a bed, already made up. Thankfully, she climbed underneath the covers after turning out the lights, trying not to listen to the sounds of the bed and the female moans coming from the bedroom. Jane knew her cheeks were bright red in the darkness of the room.

It took several minutes before exhaustion had her dozing off again. If her friends could see her right then, they would rip her a new one for placing herself in such a predicament. She missed them badly, even though she told herself she hadn't been gone for that long.

Her last thought before sleep claimed her was that she would find Bailey tomorrow, get them to the closest airport, and then get out of Mexico as fast as they could. If all went well, she would be home before her friends became really pissed. They didn't react well when they became angry.

Chapter Two

She woke up in the morning to the smell of coffee and the sight of two grim-faced women staring at her. Carina was sitting on the bed next to her, holding out a cup of coffee, while the other woman, who Jane assumed was Teresa, sat on a stool at the counter, drinking her own.

"Would you like some more sugar?"

"No, it's fine. Thank you." Jane sat up, careful not to spill the overly sweetened coffee.

"I hope you don't mind, but I told Teresa you planned to search for your sister in Peñuela."

"I don't mind—" Jane began, only to be cut off.

"You're an idiot if you think you can just walk in and then leave with her." Teresa's insult had Jane's stomach lurching as she sipped the hot coffee.

"I don't understand. Why not?"

"The Silvas are highly organized, and they don't allow

outsiders near their homes."

Jane sat undecided on her bed.

"I could go to the police."

"Who the Silvas own. They hold the power in Peñuela. No one will lift a hand to help. You will simply disappear," Teresa said matter-of-factly.

"What am I going to do?" Jane said out loud to herself.

"There may be another way," Carina's soft voice drew her attention. "Some of the men in Peñuela come to the bar on the weekend. Maybe you could ask them about your sister after they have a few drinks. It will still be dangerous, but you could find out where she is before going in blindly to find her."

Jane nodded her head, but Teresa shook hers.

"Are you crazy? If she starts asking a bunch of questions, it will be just as dangerous! They will want to know why she wants the information. She can disappear as easily here as in Peñuela."

"That is true," Carina agreed.

The women went quiet for several moments before Teresa said, "She could still work in the bar, listening. No one pays us any attention unless they want to fuck." Carina threw her room-mate a dirty look. "It's true, and you know it."

Jane watched Carina's face turn bright red. "Your fiancé?"

Teresa gave a shrill laugh. "What he doesn't know doesn't hurt him. Besides, all he cares about is the money she gives him."

"That isn't true!" Carina yelled.

"It is, but you don't want to admit it," Teresa said snidely before giving a careless shrug. "You can listen and maybe find out something that way, without drawing attention to yourself."

Jane took a drink of her now lukewarm coffee. "But I don't want to … fuck anyone."

Teresa gave another shrug. "If it gets to that point, just

motion to Carina or me, and we will take care of them. Are you sure, though? The money can be good for very little effort."

"I'm sure." Jane nodded her head empathically.

"Okay." Teresa stood up, stretching. Yawning, she set her cup down on the counter. "I need to get some sleep before tonight." With that, she left Jane and Carina alone.

"Are you sure you want to do this? You could go back and try to get the authorities there to help you."

"Would it work?"

"No."

"Then I don't have a choice, do I?"

* * *

Jane casually wiped the counter while listening to the conversations going on at the bar. She hadn't come any closer to finding Bailey; however, the little she had found out terrified her. The Silva family was heavily involved in organized crime and controlled not just one city in Mexico but several. It wasn't going to be as easy to get Bailey out as she had believed.

"Give me another beer." A loud voice drew her to the end of the bar.

Reaching for a beer under the counter, she placed it in front of the man, intending to turn away after she took his money, but his hand closed around her wrist.

"Where you going? Stay and keep me company."

Jane leaned against the counter. He was handsome, but something about him repulsed her. Maybe it was the yellow teeth or his overly tight grip on her wrist, but something about him made her want to escape. Forcing herself to relax, she gave him a smile.

"I haven't seen you in here before."

"I'm Carina's cousin." Doubt entered his eyes as he stared at her. "I grew up in El Paso and wanted to visit my mother's side of the family," Jane lied smoothly.

His doubt disappeared, and he gave her a smile, showing his yellow teeth again. "You're smart wanting to learn about your Mexican heritage. I bet you don't even want to go back home after you learned the difference between men from the States and Mexican men."

"Differences?"

"That we're better lovers." His tight grip became caressing, making her skin crawl.

"Oh."

His beady eyes narrowed on her. "You don't agree?"

"I do. I do," Jane hastily agreed yet couldn't help her next comment. "But men in the United States have bigger dicks, so I won't be staying long."

His hand stop stroking her, and he jerked her toward him, her breasts pressing flat on the counter as he tried to pull her over it. "Then let me change your mind."

Jane motioned for Teresa, who gave her an angry look as she came up beside the man who was trying to rip her arm out of its socket. "Juan, what are you doing? Are you trying to make me jealous?" Juan's scowl turned into a smile as Teresa rubbed up against him.

"No. Why would I want to make you angry, my little flower?" Jane wanted to vomit as Teresa passionately kissed Juan, rubbing her big breasts against him before pulling away teasingly.

"Go on upstairs. The door is unlocked. I'll be there in a minute." Juan was out the door in a flash.

Teresa lowered her voice to a near whisper. "If you keep making the men angry, I'm going to let you be the one to have to fuck them into a better mood. I'm getting sick of bailing your ass out of trouble."

"I'm sorry." She should have kept her mouth shut. Jane was angry at herself for placing Teresa in the position of having to bail her out of trouble again.

"Just keep your mouth shut and smile," Teresa grumbled, leaving the bar.

"What happened?" A hateful voice from behind had her turning to face her new boss.

Jorge was an asshole. He had let Teresa and Carina

convince him to let her have a job after they had gone into his private office with him. Jane didn't want to speculate what it had taken for the two women to get him to agree. Regardless, he consistently kept her under his thumb, watching every move she made as if she were going to steal the money he kept in the cash register.

When she hadn't taken any of the customers upstairs the first two nights she worked, he had wanted to fire her, but Jane had offered to take less money in pay until she was working practically for free. Jane hadn't missed the fact that, each time Carina and Teresa returned after taking a man upstairs, they would hand Jorge money.

"Nothing. Teresa was angry that I was talking to Juan."

He gave her a doubtful look before moving away.

Jane returned to cleaning the counter, looking up when she heard the bar door open. Her mouth almost dropped opened at the man entering. She had always been a woman who could appreciate a good-looking man, and that man was more than good-looking; he was outstanding.

He seemed to be in his late-twenties or early-thirties. His hair was rich brown, which set him apart from the sea of black-haired men, but it was more than that. The men in the bar all carried guns, and Jane was sure more than one had killed to get what they wanted. However, the man who had entered carried himself with lethal intent. He was tall and muscular, wearing his jeans low on his hips, with his booted feet sounding on the creaking floorboards as he walked across the room.

"Give me a whiskey." Jane nodded her head as he spoke to her in the first English she had heard in more than a week.

She stalked to the liquor bottles, automatically reaching for one that wasn't watered down. Jorge had told her to start with the hard stuff then, as they gradually became drunk, switch to the bottles he had watered down.

Her hand shook as she poured the liquor into the glass. Being careful not to spill it, she placed it before him.

"Cade! What in the hell are you doing in here?"

Jorge reached out to snatch the money from his hand before she could.

"Getting a drink. What in the fuck does it look like?" He raised the glass, taking a large swallow.

"You think that's smart after what you did?"

"What did I do?" He was talking to Jorge, but Jane felt his eyes on her. She tried to make herself look busy by drying the glasses she had washed, putting them away afterward.

"Carlos isn't going to be happy you're back in town after his guest disappeared with you."

"You mean Joe? He wanted to hitch a ride home with me, and I didn't want to make Carlos angry by refusing his friend's request."

Jorge treated the man to the same suspicious look he was constantly giving her. "That's the best story you can come up with, Cade?"

"It's the truth," he said, emptying his glass. He pushed it toward her. "Give me another one."

Jane put the towel down to refill his glass.

"You have a room I can stay in tonight?"

"I have one in the back, unless you want to stay upstairs with the women. Teresa or Carina will be happy to share their bed with you. That is, unless you can convince her." He gave a sharp nod of his head toward Jane. "Though, so far, none of the other men in here have been able to."

The asshole didn't really believe he could make her feel guilty for not wanting to have sex with the revolting men who constantly hung out in the bar, did he?

Cade's gaze slipped impassively over her body before answering. "I'll take the room out back. I need the sleep."

"Suit yourself."

Cade handed Jorge several more dollars before finishing his second drink, and then he set his glass back down on the counter. Jane couldn't help watching as he walked across the room to the hallway that had Jorge's office, the bathroom, and the spare bedroom. Jorge always kept his office locked, which Jane had learned from trying several times to get inside after Carina had told her that was where Jorge kept several addresses of the men who came in the bar.

One man in particular had come in the bar two nights ago. Carina had told her his name was Silva, and she believed he was from Peñuela. The man had talked with Jorge for quite a while at a table before leaving. She had casually tried to question the other men in the bar after he had left, only to see fear on their faces and silence at her questions. When Teresa had warned her with a silent glare, she had stopped.

Carina managed to briefly get away from a table of men she was sitting. "Cade's staying?"

Jane nodded.

"Stay away from him, Jane. Teresa doesn't even like it when I talk to him. She gets angry if she thinks you're trying to make a play for him."

"I wouldn't," Jane denied, seeing no reason to tell Carina she had been attracted to him the minute he had walked in the door.

"Jane, Teresa isn't nice. She won't play fair if she thinks you're trying to take something that's hers." Carina gripped her hand in warning. "She won't care if you get hurt."

Jane nodded, letting Carina see she would heed her warning.

She waited on tables then cleaned them down as the customers left. At the end of the night, her eyes felt heavy-lidded with fatigue as she finally climbed the steps toward the apartment.

She hadn't seen Cade for the rest of the night. Teresa had pouted the entire time after Jorge told her he was there and Cade didn't answer when she knocked on his door.

Jane was so bleary-eyed she nearly tripped over the top

step. If she didn't find out new information on her sister soon, she would have to make up her mind about whether to leave. She gave herself a time limit of two days, knowing she couldn't afford to be away too long. She had bills to pay, and her mother depended on her. Jane tried not to think about how her mother was doing without her, and then her thoughts switched to Bailey. Her sister better make this shit up to her, or Jane was going to make sure Crazy Bitch kicked her ass.

Chapter Three

Benedict looked up from his breakfast when the maid came to stand hesitantly in the doorway.

"Yes, Jana?"

"Mr. Montgomery, you have a visitor."

"Who is it?" his wife asked sharply. "Benedict, I have told you I don't like your business associates to show up here. That's why you have an office."

"I don't think they are business associates of Mr. Montgomery's," Jana said.

"I see. Whoever it is, show them to the living room, Jana." Benedict cast his wife a sharp look as he stood from the table, following behind the maid as she walked to the front door.

He went into the living room to wait, expecting one of his friends or someone with a business interest to walk through the doorway, not who did. He would rather face anyone other than the group of women staring at him with dislike.

"Where is Fat Louise?" Sex Piston didn't wait for him to greet his daughter's friends, whom he had unfortunately met on numerous occasions.

"I can't tell—"

"Bullshit." Sex Piston moved forward furiously, like a tigress protecting her cub. Benedict wished Jane's mother was as concerned. "I want to know where she is, now."

He sighed. "Ladies, have a seat."

Benedict watched as Sex Piston, T.A, Killyama, and Crazy Bitch all sat down on his large couch, staring at him as if he was the one responsible for Jane's absence.

"You are aware of Bailey's disappearance?"

"She didn't exactly disappear. The stupid bitch followed that dick she married into a fucking real life cartel story," Killyama stated harshly.

Benedict couldn't argue with her.

"We haven't seen Fat Louise for three weeks, and her dumbass mom won't tell us what's going on. She was living with Crazy Bitch, but she told us her mother wasn't feeling good and needed her to come home. When we stopped by to check on her, that bitch didn't know nothin'. If we don't get some answers, I'm going to report her missing," Sex Piston threatened.

"Don't do that!" Benedict shouted then calmed himself quickly.

"Why not?" Killyama's eyes narrowed on him.

"Because, if you do, they might not let her back into the States. I don't know if she entered Mexico legally or not."

"Oh, my God." T.A.'s mouth dropped open. "She went after that stupid bitch, didn't she?"

"I'm afraid so. I didn't know until it was too late," Benedict admitted. Their accusing gazes made him feel worthless as a father. "Her mother found the note she left behind four days after she disappeared and only contacted me when she realized she was out of money. By then, it was too late to reach her. She had already entered Mexico."

The women on the couch had been his daughter's friends for most of her life. They sat there as if they didn't know what to do or say next. That was a first for the women, he was sure.

Sex Piston was the first to recover. "What are you doing about it?"

"I've hired a man who is capable of bringing her back. If he will be successful remains to be seen. We have to remain hopeful, though."

"Fuck hope. I'm going to get her." Killyama stood up from the couch.

"No! We are not going to make this situation worse than it is. Cade will bring her back. He's the best in the business, and he has managed to complete jobs no one else has."

"Fat Louise isn't going to survive. She isn't strong enough. What's she going to do without her candy? Her favorite restaurant?" T.A. said with tears in her eyes.

"Don't say that!" Sex Piston ordered. "She is strong. Who is the one we depend on when we need shit done? She's always there for us."

The three other women nodded their heads.

Benedict felt bad for the women, aware of how close they were. Jane never went anywhere without one of the obnoxious women by her side.

"Benedict, why are they here?" Delphi came into the room, looking at the women with disdain. Benedict almost warned her; instead, he took a seat on his favorite chair to watch the fireworks.

"You the bitch who's always putting Fat Louise down?" Crazy Bitch asked.

"Fat Louise? You're still calling each other childish nicknames?"

"Delphi," Benedict warned, trying to put an end to the heightened tension that had begun when his wife entered the room.

"You don't mind them being so rude?"

Benedict shrugged. He had learned to deal with it long ago.

"You pretentious—" Sex Piston began, but Benedict decided to end the confrontation before it really began. If they decided to attack Delphi, he wouldn't be able to pull them off her by himself.

"Perhaps you should go ahead and leave for your hair appointment," he suggested.

"Very well." His wife curled her lip, turning to leave the room, but was brought up short by Killyama blocking the doorway.

"I know you're the reason Fat Louise took off after that stuck-up daughter of yours. She told me you were pulling a guilt trip on her, and I told her she should shove a fucking foot up your ass. If something happens to her, you're not going to miss that daughter of yours, because I'm going to send you there in a fucking casket."

Delphi's hand went to her throat in shock at the warning. "Are you going to let this … this … trash talk to me that way?"

"Actually, it's what I've been thinking myself," Benedict said without sympathy.

Delphi brushed by Killyama, leaving the room, although not without a fearful glance back at the women.

After they heard the slamming of the front door, Benedict returned his attention to Jane's friends. "Go home. I'll contact you as soon as I hear something from Cade."

Most of the group stood then walked out of the room with worried expressions. However, Killyama stayed where she was, giving him a glacial stare that nearly curled his balls in fear.

"You let Fat Louise's mom and that bitch of a wife treat her like shit. If anything happens to her, that bitch won't be the only one I come after."

"You're not going to wait to hear from me, are you?"

"What do you fucking think?"

Benedict was left staring at the empty doorway. He almost felt sorry for Mexico if that woman was headed their way.

Chapter Four

"Wake up!" The command was followed by a brutal punch to her ribs, startling Jane awake. Her frightened eyes lifted to the soldier staring down furiously at her. Despite the pain in her side, she jumped to her feet. Seeing another soldier in the doorway raised her alarm even further.

Jane saw Carina and Teresa standing in their bedroom doorway with terror on their faces.

"Que haces aquí?" She couldn't understand a word he said. Her sleep-fogged mind couldn't translate the words fast enough.

Frowning, he repeated the sentence in English. "What are you doing here?"

Jane thought quickly. "I'm visiting my cousin." She gave a nod towards Carina.

The two soldiers stared at her skeptically.

"I don't see the family resemblance." He took her face

in his large hand, his grip hurting like hell, but she didn't try to pull away.

"We're, like, fourth cousins," Jane lied. "I wanted to learn more about my heritage." The soldier's hand dropped away.

"Why have you been asking about the Silvas?"

"My mother mentioned them. I was trying to find out if we may have a familia connection." The men talked quietly before bursting into laughter.

The one pointing a gun on her lowered it to his side. "That may be possible. The Silvas like to spread their seed."

Jane didn't like the way the two men were staring at her. She became aware of her thin nightgown, crossing her arms over her breasts.

"Grab your things. We will take you to meet more of your family."

"I've talked to my mother. I had the name wrong. I'm related to the Villas."

"I can see how you would be confused." All amusement disappeared. "Get your things."

Jane thought about getting her backpack with the gun in it yet didn't like her chances. Instead, she swallowed hard. "I really don't want to go with you."

"I don't give a fuck what you want." The man who had woken her by punching her pushed her towards the doorway. All of them came to a stop when they saw the man standing bare-chested in the doorway.

"Don't have anything better to do besides trying to kidnap a woman out of her bed, Luis?"

"Cade!" The bastard took a step forward, holding out his hand for Cade to shake. "Where have you been, you hijo de puta?"

"Been busy, but not as busy as you."

Jane tried not to stare at his chest. She should be scared shitless; instead, she had to force her eyes upward, her arousal spiking.

He didn't even glance her way, keeping his attention focused on the soldiers.

"Her? She was just going to be a plaything for Javier tonight. He gets bored easily."

"He must be for you to take her to him. From what I remember about him, she's hardly his taste."

Luis turned back to stare pointedly at Jane's breasts, which were easily visible under the sheer gown.

"He's right." The one holding the rifle lifted the bottom of her gown to her thighs with the barrel of his gun. "She doesn't have enough meat on her."

"Let's get a drink." Cade moved to go back down the steps.

Luis paused before motioning for the other soldier to leave. The gown fell back down her thighs.

"You should search somewhere else for your family ties," Luis's harsh warning had her trembling.

She nodded her understanding, sinking back down onto her bed. Carina ran forward slamming and locking the door.

"Estúpido perra! I told you to be careful," Teresa hissed at her, not moving from the bedroom doorway.

"I'm sorry. I thought I was. I'll leave." Jane stood to her feet.

"You can't. It's the middle of the night," Carina protested.

"I don't want to put you or Teresa in danger."

"We're not the one in danger. Those men know they can have us, that our families are not wealthy. We would serve no purpose. You, on the other hand, could pose a threat to them with your questions, and they will eliminate any threats to their organization," Teresa told her, going back into the bedroom and slamming the door closed.

"I'll leave on the bus in the morning."

Carina shook her head. "Give it one more day. We will try harder to get into Jorge's office. Maybe you can find something to help you. He's been in business a long time.

Surely, he will have the address of someone in the Silva family."

Jane gave in. She needed an address, and most of the legal addresses given were not the ones they lived in; using fake addresses as a way to keep their residence a secret from their enemies was common practice.

"Are you okay?"

Jane nodded her head, not mentioning the soreness of her ribs. The violence of the situation had her shuddering. If Cade hadn't shown up, she was sure the soldiers would have taken her. She had stayed too long.

"I'm fine, but I need to leave before they decide to come back."

"I think so, too." Carina agreed unhappily. "Tomorrow, we'll find something to help you."

"I hope so." Jane lay back down on the bed after Carina left her. Covering herself with the blanket, she buried her face in the pillow.

She had never missed her friends more. In hindsight, Jane wished she had confided in them. Although she had made a mistake not doing so, she wasn't going to call them to help her. She wouldn't endanger her friends because of Bailey. Her sister was her responsibility.

"I'll find her, and when I do, I'll be able to go home," Jane promised, brushing a tear away. She was homesick and scared.

Taking a deep breath, she brought images of her friends to her mind, which eased her anxiety. Even hundreds of miles away, they gave her strength enough to close her eyes and go to sleep.

* * *

Jane dressed for work in her borrowed clothes from Carina. She hurried, wanting to be downstairs during lunch since it would be the best time to search Jorge's office. She went downstairs, going through the back door to the small kitchen behind the bar. Jorge didn't provide much food to the bar customers, mainly items he bought from vendors that could be easily reheated.

She grabbed a tamale from the metal pan sitting on top of the stove. Taking a bite, she enjoyed the spicy flavor.

"Jorge will make you pay for that," Carina teased, coming inside the kitchen to place some dishes in the sink.

Jane made a face. "On my salary, I'll owe him for letting me work here."

"Do you need some money? I can lend you some," she offered.

Jane shook her head. "No, I'm fine." She wouldn't take the money from her friend; she worked too hard for it.

Jane and Carina went into the barroom where Carina waited on tables while Jane worked behind the bar. When she had started working at the bar, she had been slow, but now she moved back and forth behind the bar with familiarity. When she returned home, she might take a part time job bartending.

She saw Teresa sitting at a table with Cade. He was wearing a black T-shirt, and his wet hair made it look as if he had just taken a shower. Every so often, Teresa would get up to refill his drink or get him food. Jane tried not to watch them as she worked; however, Cade was hard not to notice. She wanted to smack herself for staring at them.

Bringing herself back to earth, she started focusing on Jorge. He seemed tired today, moving slowly behind the bar as he helped waiting on customers.

Seeing his keys were on the shelf next to the glasses, she took several glasses and placed them carefully on the shelf. She glanced around quickly to make sure no one was paying attention to her, and then she slid the keys into her pocket.

"Jorge, I'm not feeling well. I need to go to the restroom." Jane told him as he moved from one customer to the next.

He studied her face for a second before nodding. "Hurry the fuck up. We're busy."

Jane guessed fear of getting caught taking his keys had

made her face pale, adding credibility to her claim.

"I'll try." Jane tried to give a make-believe sick look before disappearing around the corner where his office was. The bathroom was directly in front of it, and the room that Cade was renting was next to it.

Jane hurriedly slipped the key in the door after checking to make sure no one else was near. Slipping inside, she closed and locked the door in relief. She stared around the office in dismay. It was filled with papers and boxes. She would never be able to find anything in here before Jorge noticed she had been gone for too long.

Taking a deep breath to calm herself, she began her search, making sure to place things back exactly as they were so Jorge wouldn't know she had searched his things. Time flew and Jane was about to give up when she noticed a ledger lying on top of a box that was closest to his desk. Opening it, she saw several names with money amounts and addresses.

Jane ran her finger down the column, almost shouting when she saw the last name Silva. Jane memorized the address then closed the ledger.

Barely opening the door, she peeked outside, and seeing no one, she slipped back out into the hallway. She was about to close the door when she found herself jerked away as a hand reached out and snapped the door closed.

Jane stared up into Cade's face as she was backed against the now closed door with Cade plastered against her.

"What?" Before she could say anything else, his mouth slammed down on hers. Jane's hands pressed against his chest as she tried to turn her head to the side. A firm hand on the side of her face held her still as his tongue pressed against the seam of her lips. Unable to stop herself, Jane parted her lips, letting him enter. Her hands fluttered against his chest before grabbing on to his T-shirt to steady herself. His tongue slid against hers in an intimate way that had her wanting to imitate the movement.

"What the fuck, Cade? You already have one of my girls. I need at least one to work. Carina's upstairs with a customer. Either pick Teresa or Jane." Jorge stomped back around the corner. When he moved, Jane saw a furious Teresa staring at her from the end of the hallway.

Cade took a step away, giving her room to move. Jane hurried forward, intending to go back to work, but Teresa blocked her path. Carina had warned her about Teresa's fury.

"Teresa, come here." The male voice behind her had a seductive pitch that had Jane's head turning, but Cade wasn't looking at her. His attention was on Teresa, who nearly knocked her over when she brushed by. Jane's mouth dropped open at her rudeness while Cade's arms slid around Teresa's waist as she neared him, pulling her closer to him. When Teresa lifted her mouth to his, Jane spun around and left the two alone.

"Why am I not surprised he picked Teresa?" Jorge's sarcastic comment had Jane's blood boiling.

"Maybe because she's a slut?" Jane snapped, handing a customer a fresh beer.

Jorge raised his brow at her yet didn't say anything else. Jane tried not to notice that neither Cade nor Teresa immediately returned to the bar. She tried not to let it bother her, but somehow, it did.

It was over an hour before Teresa returned to the bar, shooting her a triumphant look, which she ignored. Setting down the bar rag, she walked to Jorge's side. "I'm going upstairs for a break. I'm still not feeling well."

"Go," he snapped. "Make sure you're back before six."

"I will," Jane lied. She had no intentions of ever stepping foot in the bar again.

She felt inexplicitly sad that she would never see Cade again, which made no sense, considering she didn't even know him.

"For Christ's sake, I've never even talked to him," she said to herself. Her anger at herself didn't make her feel better, even though she told herself it did.

Before she walked out, Carina gave her a sad smile, somehow knowing Jane wouldn't be coming back. Jane gave her a thumbs up in return as she passed. She would leave Carina a note, thanking her for her help. Jane would miss the friendship that had begun yet promised herself she would keep in touch.

As she headed upstairs, Jane looked down at her watch. She had twenty minutes to catch the bus for Peñuela. She was going to find her sister and get back to the life she had left behind.

Chapter Five

"Going somewhere?"

Jane dropped the shirt she was stuffing into her backpack.

Cade was standing in the bedroom doorway, putting on his T-shirt. Jane turned bright red. Teresa must have brought him upstairs using the back steps and had left him in her bed when she returned downstairs.

"I'm leaving, heading back to the States. I was visiting Carina, but now my vacation's over." Jane picked the shirt back up, shoving it inside the backpack then zipping it closed. She didn't look at him as she sat down to pull on the tennis shoes Carina had given her.

Ignoring Cade, she set an envelope down on the kitchen counter with her goodbye note and some money to cover the cost of the clothes she had been given.

"Where are you really going, Jane? Your family will be

happy to hear you're heading home, but I don't believe that's where you're going, is it?"

She stopped mid-stride, turning to face him. She started to reply yet was cut off.

"Don't lie. You're a lousy liar. I'm not in the mood to listen to you make up another one."

"You should be in a good mood after just getting laid," Jane snapped.

Cade grinned at her. "It cost me a hundred bucks, and I'm going to get my money back from your father for a business expense."

Jane's eyes widened when he mentioned her father as if he knew him.

"My father?"

Cade nodded his head, coming farther into the room. "He hired me to find you and your sister. He wants you both back in the States."

Jane felt her eyes fill with tears. "Daddy sent you?"

"Yeah, Daddy sent me. Christ, how have you managed not to get yourself killed yet?"

Jane's shoulders straightened. "There's no need to be sarcastic." Her eyes narrowed on him. "How do I know my father sent you to help?"

"You don't. You'll just have to trust me, won't you?"

Jane could tell from his expression he really didn't care if she believed him or not.

"How did you find me?"

"The cell phone you have hidden in your backpack puts out a nice, clear signal for me to follow."

"How did you know it was in my backpack...?" Jane's voice trailed off as she guessed he had been snooping after Teresa left.

"Let's go. I want to get out of here."

Jane nodded, sliding the strap of her backpack onto her shoulder.

"We're going to Peñuela?"

"I'm going to Peñuela. I'm dropping you off at an

airstrip. A buddy of mine will fly you back to an airport where your father can pick you up."

Jane shook her head. "I'm going with you to find Bailey."

"Nope." Cade took her arm, leading her to the door.

She jerked away. "I'm not going home without her."

"You don't have a fucking choice. I'm not taking you to Peñuela. It'll be easier for me to get Bailey out without having to try to keep up with you. Use your common sense!"

Jane hated to admit he was right. "How do I know I can trust you to save my sister?"

"Again, you don't." He shrugged. "But there's no other choice. You're lucky I was here last night, or Luis would have taken you to Javier. Believe me, you don't want to meet Javier."

"I don't?"

"No, you don't. Now, can we fucking go?"

"Yes," Jane gave in, wanting to go home. If her father had hired Cade, he would find her sister and get her out safer than she could. Jane knew her limitations, and she had definitely passed those last night.

Cade followed her down the steps, motioning for her to go towards the small parking lot where there were several vehicles. Jane tried to guess which one was his yet lost when he opened the door to an old, grey Chevy. Jane climbed inside, wincing when he slammed the door shut.

Cade sat down behind the wheel after shutting his own door. He drove out of the lot, heading away from the bar.

"I thought yours was the SUV." Cade threw her a surprised look, as though he couldn't understand what she was talking about. Jane blushed slightly. "I tried to guess which vehicle was yours. I guessed wrong."

"This isn't my truck. I bought it from Jorge. I wouldn't drive an expensive SUV like that."

"Why not?" she asked curiously.

"Because it would get stolen at the first roadblock. This

piece of shit, no one will want. I had to give Jorge a thousand for it."

"Another business expense?"

"That's right."

"This is going to cost my father a lot of money, isn't it?"

"He can afford it," he said without sympathy.

"Yes, he can, but sleeping with Teresa doesn't count as a business expense," Jane snapped back, becoming tired of his unfriendly attitude. People were usually nice to her. Actually, the only people who didn't like her were her stepmother, her sister, Teresa, and The Last Riders. But everyone else liked her. She was a nice person and went out of her way to make people freaking like her. She shouldn't take it personally. Maybe he was an asshole who didn't like anyone.

"Yes, it does. It was hard work to satisfy her. Teresa would have turned you over to the Silvas if she became angry enough. She was mad as hell when she saw me kissing you."

"Why did you kiss me?" Jane asked, making sure not to look at him when she asked.

"Jorge was about five steps behind me. If he had seen you come out of his office, he would have shot you and thrown your dead body out his back door."

"He wouldn't have shot me!"

Cade gave her a grim look that had her believing him.

"He would have?"

"Yes. Jorge might come off as a bumbling idiot, but he takes his own safety seriously. He wouldn't have let you jeopardize his safety for any reason. That's how he's kept alive all these years."

Jane stared out the window, watching the people in the streets as they passed. They walked on the sidewalk like they would in any city, although they dealt with the fear of getting killed daily.

Cade drove through the city. Gradually, it thinned out

until they were driving on a smaller two-lane road. Jane began to get nervous when he drove onto a small, dirt road.

"This is the way to the airport?"

"We're going to an airstrip. There's a difference."

"There is?"

"Yes. Fuck!" Cade gradually began to slow the truck down.

"What's wrong?" Jane asked.

Cade nodded his head toward the road in front of them. "There's a roadblock."

Jane's breath hitched. She had been stopped while on the buses a couple of times, each one terrifying her.

"Stay quiet and do everything they tell you."

Jane nodded as he stopped the truck.

"Get out." A soldier dressed in fatigues pointed a gun at Cade. Cade held his hands in the air and carefully reached down to open his truck door. The soldier kept his gun pointed on Cade as they climbed out of the truck. Jane's own hands rose into the air when she saw another soldier standing by the truck-bed with a gun trained on her.

"There is a toll for traveling on this road. Give me your money," Jane heard the soldier demand from Cade.

She turned to watch as Cade pulled the cash from his pocket, handing it to the soldier who shoved it into his own pocket.

"Is that all you have?"

"Yes." Cade's voice was low and non-confrontational. Jane was kind of surprised, thinking he would have fought harder to keep his money.

"Search the truck." The soldier motioned her to go stand beside Cade as he opened the truck door.

Jane stood beside Cade as the soldier found her backpack, pulling it out of the truck to toss it to the ground in front of the soldier who had taken Cade's cash. He bent down, tossing her clothes in the dirt as he shifted through her things. He stared up at her in surprise when he pulled out the gun before shoving it into the waistband of his pants. Standing up, he kicked the backpack towards her, and she bent to pick it up.

"Get out of here."

After Jane and Cade both got back inside the truck, Cade made a turn and went back the direction they had come from.

"We're not going to the landing strip?"

"Change of plan. I don't have the money to pay the pilot, and he doesn't do credit. I'll find a place for us to stay in Peñuela and get some more cash. Looks like you'll be flying back with your sister after all."

Jane was both relieved and frustrated. She had wanted this ordeal to be over, but she was relieved not to be going back without Bailey. She hadn't liked feeling like she had failed her father.

Sometime later, Jane announced, "I'm hungry."

"How am I supposed to pay for food?" Cade replied.

Jane took her shoe off and pulled out some folded money, showing it to him.

Cade's eyes glinted with anger. "It would have been good to know you had that money before I missed the plane."

"It's not a lot, but it should be enough to buy me something to eat," Jane snapped back angrily.

Cade's lips tightened as he slowed the truck down to turn into a store.

"Stay here."

Jane regretted telling him she was hungry, but dammit, she was. He was the rudest man she had ever met. Even The Last Riders weren't rude to her. They were rude to the rest of her friends yet ignored her like everyone else did.

She glumly took the hotdog and soda from Cade when he returned. "Thank you." Jane hoped he didn't hear her sniffle.

"What the hell is wrong with you?" he said, backing the

truck up. "I thought you would be happy to go with me to find Bailey. I even fed you, and you look like I shot your fucking dog."

"You don't have to be so freaking rude," Jane said, taking a bite of the hotdog.

Cade turned back to face the road, but for a second, she thought she saw a brief softening in his expression. Then he blew it with his next comment.

"Just eat the fucking hotdog."

Asshole.

Chapter Six

Jane stood at the hotel window, staring out. They had been there for two days, sharing the same room. He had slept on the small couch, while she had taken the bed. It had been miserable.

Cade had left her behind to scout the address she had found to see if Bailey could possibly be there. Jane prayed she was. If not, she hoped it would at least lead to where she was being kept. Jane wished it could be as simple for Cade to find Bailey as it had been her; however, Bailey's phone hadn't worked since she had entered Mexico. Jane's own phone was now useless until she could purchase a charger, and since Cade had taken all her money, that wasn't going to be anytime soon.

Several men walking down the street caught her attention. Something about one of them seemed familiar. Jane's breath caught in her throat as she practically pressed her face to the glass. It was Raul! He was with three other men who were talking as they paused outside a bar. Jane was tempted to leave the hotel and run across the street to demand to see her sister, but she didn't. Sex Piston or Killyama would, even Crazy Bitch would. T.A. would without thinking about it, yet Jane merely stared stupidly out the window, wishing Cade would come back.

Ultimately deciding to be more proactive, Jane braced herself and picked up the truck keys from the nightstand. Then she practically ran outside, afraid the men would leave before she could get inside the truck. Trying to appear inconspicuous, she slowed her pace to the truck, opened it, and climbed behind the steering wheel to wait.

Raul was the first to leave, and Jane prayed he didn't look her way. Thankfully, he turned in the opposite direction. Jane waited until he turned the corner before starting the truck. Slowly pulling out, she drove at a snail's pace down the road, turning the corner where she saw him get into a black SUV. Jane pulled over and parked the truck.

The SUV pulled out, and Jane waited until it was almost out of sight before pulling out again. She bit her lip as she followed, already regretting the decision to follow Raul. Cade would be furious with her.

She turned at a bend in the road and gave a frightened squeak when she saw the roadblock. She wanted to turn around, but there was another dark SUV coming up behind her, pinning her between the two vehicles.

Jane watched helplessly as Raul remained in his vehicle and talked to the soldiers. One broke away and walked toward the truck she was sitting inside.

"Get out."

Jane shakily stepped out of the truck, trying to keep her back toward Raul's SUV. She didn't have to be told she had made a terrible mistake leaving the hotel.

"Give me your cash." The soldier made no pretense of collecting a toll.

"I ... I don't have any."

She went flying backwards against the truck when a hand suddenly hit her across the face. Jane barely managed to put her hands up to protect herself before another strike landed on her.

"Please, I don't have any money. If I did, I would give it to you," Jane pleaded as a harsh hand grabbed her by the hair and pulled her toward him.

"Then I guess you will be paying in something other than cash." His hand went to her T-shirt, and Jane felt the material rip at his sharp movement.

"Diego, stop." Raul came to stand next to her.

When the men in the SUV behind them also got out and came forward, Jane knew she was in more trouble than she could handle.

"Let her go. That is my sister-in-law you plan on raping." Jane's frightened eyes met Raul's cruel ones. "What are you doing here, Jane?"

"I thought I would come for a visit," Jane said mockingly.

"Bailey didn't tell me you were coming."

"I wanted it to be a surprise. Surprise!" Jane said lamely.

Raul didn't try to hide his distaste for her antics. "You can ride the rest of the way with my men. Diego, get rid of the truck."

"Wait, I'll need that when I leave."

"No, you won't. You won't be leaving." Raul turned, leaving her to his men.

After one of the men took her arm, leading her to the SUV and practically throwing her inside, Jane straightened on the seat. She had been constantly manhandled since she had entered Mexico. The women in the States would drag these Neanderthals to court if they were handled the way she had been.

One of the other soldiers moved the truck she had been driving, letting them pass.

Cade was going to kill her when he found her. Jorge was going to be pissed his truck wouldn't be returned. This whole debacle was a huge failure.

* * *

Cade stared around the empty room, his hands clenched into fists. He strode angrily to the nightstand, seeing the truck keys gone.

"Motherfucker!" He went back downstairs where the desk clerk gave him a frightened look when he stormed up to the desk.

"Have you seen the woman who was with me?"

"She left about an hour ago. I saw her drive that way." He pointed outside the grimy window in the direction she had taken.

"Did she leave a message for me?"

"No, she didn't say anything. She was running very fast."

"She was running?" His anger turned to worry.

The clerk nodded.

"Was anyone chasing her?"

"No."

Cade's anger returned with a vengeance. He was going to strangle her. He had told her to stay in the hotel room.

Turning on his heel, he headed out of the hotel. He took his cell phone out of his pocket and called Luis.

"I need a favor," he said as soon as Luis answered.

"Depends on what it is."

"I need something to drive and cash. Can you make it happen?"

"Si. Give me thirty minutes. Where are you?"

Cade gave him the address then disconnected the call. He glanced up and down the street then back at the hotel. He had thirty minutes to find out what had caused her to run from the hotel. If he didn't find her, he had basically lost a hundred thousand dollars, and he didn't fucking like losing money.

He refused to acknowledge that money wasn't the only

43

reason he was furious at Jane for being gone. She was just another job. That was all. He would find her and return her to her father. She would never cross his mind again. Thank God for that because she was a pain in his ass, constantly complaining about being hungry, thinking she was too good to talk to him. What's more, when he told her to stay put, did she? Hell no!

Bitch!

Chapter Seven

Jane laid her head down on her knees. She was sitting on the bed with her knees pulled up to her chest in a luxurious bedroom she had been locked in for two days.

When she heard the door open, she raised her head, thinking someone was bringing her lunch. The only time anyone entered was to bring her a tray of food.

"Bailey!" Jane jumped off the bed, running toward her sister.

When she would have hugged her, Bailey coldly sidestepped Jane, setting down a small suitcase she was carrying.

"Why are you here?"

Jane stared in dismay at her younger sister. "I came to help you. Dad and your mother were worried when you told them Raul wouldn't let you leave."

"I over-exaggerated a bit. We had a small fight." She

shrugged. "Now we've made up."

"Then why haven't you called?" Jane looked her sister over carefully. She didn't look like she had been hurt or was in distress. In fact, she looked fucking fantastic. "Why haven't you come to see me before now? I've been here for two days!"

"I've been busy."

Jane wanted to smack her sister.

"I had to take off work. I've spent days traveling to get here. I even worked in a bar." Jane took a deep breath. "And you're too fucking busy to come to my room in the same house you're living in?"

"I don't live here. This is Javier's home, Raul's uncle."

"Oh." That made Jane feel marginally better. She could have lived in another city, and it might have taken time to get her here.

"We live a mile away. Our house was the first one on the road."

Jane remembered seeing the huge house as they drove past. She could have walked to see her.

"Fine. I'm glad you're okay. I'll tell Dad and your mother. Now, will you please ask your husband to give me a ride back to my hotel? I want to go home."

Bailey waved a hand dismissively at her request. "Raul wants you to stay and visit for a while, so I brought you a few clothes since Raul told me you didn't bring any. You really should have come better prepared."

"But I want to go home. I need to get back to work," Jane argued. "I didn't bring any clothes, because I didn't plan on getting kidnapped."

"Your job can wait. Raul wants you to stay, so you'll just have to stay." Bailey ignored Jane's angry face. "Besides, you weren't kidnapped. You were the one chasing after Raul."

"Bailey, you're married to the man, so it's your choice if you want to listen to his lies, but I don't have to. I think it's crazy, and I want to leave."

"It's different here in Mexico. Here, women respect their husbands."

Jane wanted to vomit. "No, it's not. What's different is your willingness to put up with this bullshit."

Bailey's pretty face flushed with anger. "I never could talk to you!"

"You could always talk to me. You just never wanted to, because I'm not going to just spout off shit to make you happy. Bailey, I'm telling you this is a fucked up situation."

"I don't have time for this. Some of my friends are coming over for dinner tonight. Our husbands are having a business meeting, so we're having a get-together. I'll see you in a few days. Maybe you will have calmed down by then." Her sister turned to the door.

"Don't you dare leave me!"

Bailey gave her a smug glance before going out the door, slamming it shut behind her.

"Bailey!" Jane frantically tried to open the door, only to find it was locked. "Bailey!" She wasn't coming back.

Jane leaned on the wooden door, wanting to bang her head against it for being stupid enough to try to help her sister. Finally, her knees gave out, and she slid to the floor, wanting to scream and rant at the closed door. Instead, she fought back silent tears.

The only small thread of hope she held on to was that Cade would find her. Without that thought keeping her calm, Jane didn't know what she would do. He was her last hope of returning home.

By the next day, she had lost that hope, though. She was going to take her escape into her own hands. She had put herself in this situation; therefore, she would get herself out.

Jane waited until it was dark and her dinner had been brought in before slipping on a pair of jeans as well as a long-sleeved shirt that had been in the suitcase Bailey had given her and putting on her tennis shoes.

The door was locked, but someone always returned to pick up her tray. Jane was so nervous she barely tasted it, but without knowing when her next meal would be, she forced each tasteless bite down until she had eaten the whole meal. She set the plates to the side then went to stand by the door, tensely waiting. After what seemed like hours, she heard the key turn in the door.

Jane waited only long enough to see the dark head of a soldier before bringing the tray down on his head. Thinking fast, she grabbed the key from where he had dropped it when she struck him. He was trying to regain his footing when Jane struck him with the tray again. This time, he fell down face forward and didn't get back up.

She stuck her head out of the doorway, making sure no one else was there, before walking out and closing the door behind her, locking it for good measure. Let the bastard see how easy it was to get out of the locked room.

Jane's instinct was to run like hell, but reason had her walking slowly down the steps she had been brought up. She heard loud voices to the side and knew she wouldn't be able to slip past to the front door without being seen.

Cautiously, she moved toward the back of the house. Most houses had back doors, and she prayed this one wasn't any different. Smelling food, she knew she was heading in the direction of the kitchen, which Jane feared would have servants. She stopped for a moment, trying to think of her best option, then realized she didn't need a door to escape.

She saw a door to her left, and taking a fearful breath, she opened it slowly, her eyes widening when she saw the contents. Ducking into the room, she closed the door behind her. There were guns everywhere along with several boxes lying on tables, which Jane took valuable time to search, and she was glad she had.

Jane picked up a wicked looking knife, shoving it in the back of her pants before pulling her shirt over it. Then she picked out a gun that seemed similar to the one John had shown her how to use, praying it was loaded. She promised herself she was going to take a shooting class when she returned home, but then changed her mind. She would beg Stud to teach her, instead. This was the last time she would find herself in this situation.

Opening another box, her brow wrinkled into a frown. It couldn't contain what she thought they were. Gingerly, she took one out and placed it in her pocket before she looked around and found a canvas ammo bag to put a couple more into. She didn't know if the bullets inside would work with the gun she held but when she found a safe location she would see if they would fit in the chamber.

Opening the door again, Jane peeked out. When she didn't see anyone, she edged into the hallway, quietly closing the door behind her. She then cautiously opened the door next to the one she had just left, finding it dark inside. Trying to quiet her loud breathing, it was a few minutes before she felt in control again.

Her heart almost skipped a beat when she saw moonlight glinting into the dark room from a window. She carefully walked across the room, bumping her knees several times on furniture. At last, she reached the window, expecting to hear the loud sound of an alarm as she raised it, and prepared to throw herself out of it if she did. However, the only sound she heard was the sound of loud laughter coming from the front of the house. If there was an alarm, it must have been cut off while the party was going on.

Jane sat on the ledge of the window before easing herself out. Once outside, she tried to determine which would be the best direction to go. She was at the back of the house, facing another smaller house several feet away with a lit path leading the way up to it. Jane was afraid to go to the front of that house, worried she would be spotted by someone from the other house who would then alert Raul.

Suddenly, Jane heard the sound of a door opening and ran to hide in the shadows of the house, crouching down behind several thick bushes. Raul's uncle had obviously spent a fortune on landscaping.

She watched as a large group of men walked down the path toward the smaller house. The man in the lead was dressed expensively in a suit, and the other men followed him deferentially, as if he were royalty. He held a lit cigarette in his hand, and Jane shivered as he brought the smoking tube to his lips. The brief flare highlighted his sensuously cruel features as he talked to his men.

Raul gazed with admiration at the man, making Jane wonder if he were Raul's uncle, Javier. He flicked his cigarette to the ground before stepping on it, continuing to the house where he paused to knock on the door.

A soldier opened it, standing back to let the men enter. As the door began to close, Jane prepared herself to make a run for the front of the house until a loud scream filled the night.

The door was thrown wide open, and a young woman ran out of the house with a terrified expression on her face.

Horrorstricken, Jane saw Raul come back outside, catching the woman halfway down the path by her hair flying out behind her before dragging her to a stop. Her screams intensified until Raul slapped her across the mouth several times, quieting the woman. Raul didn't release the woman's hair, using it to drag her back inside the house, instead. Then a soldier came out and closed the door behind him before standing guard.

Jane sank to her ass in defeat. She couldn't go anywhere until the guard went back inside.

It wasn't in her personality to stay quiet. Under normal circumstances, she would call the cops or her friends to get help. Here, the police didn't help, her friends were nowhere near, and if she tried to take on the men alone, she would lose.

The men disgusted her, and she was afraid she wouldn't be able to hide if she kept hearing the screams coming from inside the house.

Many, many times over the years, she had wished she had the personalities of her friends. They were all ball-busters, not afraid of anything, whereas she usually hid among them. They had protected her since she was a kid, and she had become used to it. Without them by her side, she felt lost and alone. If Killyama was there, she would have raised the gun in her hand and shot the guard before saving the woman whose cries were breaking her heart.

When Raul finally opened the door again, his shirt had been removed and his pants were unbuttoned He said something to the guard, and then the two turned and entered the small house, closing the door behind them.

Jane's heart accelerated. Now would be the perfect opportunity to slip away. She planned out in her head how she would sneak through the grounds parallel to the road. That's when the screams from inside escalated.

She couldn't stop herself from leaving her hiding place to steal across the yard until she was scrunched down next to the small house where she peered through a side window. Her hand pressed against her mouth to stifle her own scream of revulsion. Raul was standing over the helpless woman removing his pants, Jane saw more of her brother-in-law than she ever wanted to see, he had a tattoo of two pistols framing his cock. Jane felt like scrubbing her eyeballs to remove the picture from her mind.

The pretty little house on the outside hid the ugliness within. It was one large room with several beds the men were making use of as they raped many women. The one Raul was raping must have been giving him too much trouble, because the guard was holding her down for him. The one Jane thought was Javier was standing, watching his men commit the atrocities against the helpless women.

Fuck it; she couldn't watch any longer. Jane raised the gun, pointing it at Raul's thrusting ass, when a hand covered her mouth, jerking her backward and dragging her away from the house. Terrified, she struggled to bring the gun up to shoot whoever was carrying her into the dark shadows.

"Stop fighting me," Cade hissed. "I'm trying to save your ass."

Tears of relief flooded her eyes. She had managed to escape herself, but it was nice not being alone.

"We have to go back and help them!" Jane whispered furiously.

"We can't help them without getting ourselves killed." Cade took her arm, leaving her no choice except to walk away from the house of horrors.

"I can't leave them!"

"We have no choice. Do you see a SWAT team to back us up? Javier has turned his house into a military stronghold. I had to call in a favor or I would never have found this place." Cade dropped her arm. "If you try to help them, you'll get them killed. At least they stand a chance of surviving when he sells them."

"He sells them?"

"Javier sells everything. He'd sell his own mother if he thought someone would buy her."

"Where are we going?" Jane asked, hating herself for leaving those women behind.

"We're going to get your sister and get the fuck out of here."

Chapter Eight

"She won't want to leave. She's completely blinded by Raul."

"Then we're going to enlighten her. I haven't busted my ass for half a payday."

Jane tried not to let his words bother her, but it stung being reminded the only reason he was there was for money.

"Do you always have to be such an ass?"

"Yeah." He held up his hand, motioning for her to be quiet. "Follow my lead."

Jane watched as he peeked around the corner then began to maneuver across the grounds. She followed on his heels, dodging into the shadows of trees and staying still until he moved again. She was relieved when they were behind the house Bailey had described as hers. They went to the back door where Cade knocked quietly.

"How do you know she's alone?" Jane whispered.

"I scouted here first before I went to Javier's house."

He tapped on the door several times before Bailey appeared.

Her frightened eyes saw Cade first. When Jane could tell she was about to scream, she stepped out from behind Cade.

"Let us in, Bailey."

Bailey's eyes widened, opening the door wider yet blocking the doorway with her body.

"Jane, what are you doing here?" She didn't try to lower her voice.

"Shh! Let us in." Jane wanted to reach out and shake her sister when she hesitated, but then Bailey moved back, letting them walk inside.

"What are you doing here?" she repeated as soon as Jane and Cade were both inside. "Who are you?" she asked Cade.

"I came to get you out!" Jane snapped. "He's Cade. Dad sent him to help us."

"Are you crazy? I'm not leaving my husband," Bailey hissed.

Jane's mouth dropped open. "You're serious? You wrote Dad…" Jane had held out hope that her behavior at Javier's house had been because they might have been overheard. It appeared her sister had been serious, though.

Bailey shrugged. "I was scared at first. Now, I'm not. Raul has assured me everyone is very friendly toward American women, and I've even made several friends," she boasted.

"Are you fucking insane?" Jane was almost yelling at her sister then regretted her words. Bailey was difficult to deal with under normal circumstances, and she never liked to feel as if she was in the wrong.

"I'm not leaving. You both need to leave before Raul gets back and finds you here."

"Fine. Let's go," Cade said, moving toward the door.

"I'm not leaving without Bailey," Jane refused.

Turning back to her sister, she implored, "How can you want to stay here? Are you deaf as well as blind to what's going on around here? They are hurting women!"

The screams from the women couldn't be heard inside Bailey's home, but sound traveled, and the men didn't seem worried about quieting the women's screams. The houses were close enough that Jane would bet Bailey had heard them before.

"Raul explained that to me. It's their culture. They admire power, and violence here is an expected response to challenges of power."

"The women they are holding hostage in that house aren't challenging them. They just want to get away from their rapists."

"They're not raping them; their courting them." Bailey waved her hand. "Raul explained it to me."

Jane's mouth dropped open. At that point, she almost left her sister. If not for her father and stepmother's anguish, she would have.

"Those women are being raped! They are being used as sex slaves. No woman in their right mind would believe anything else."

Bailey paled. "But Raul told me—"

"Is Raul courting another woman?" Jane interrupted. "Because I saw him go inside the house and rape a woman who barely looked eighteen."

"You're wrong. Raul wouldn't have touched those women. Maybe he was trying to stop them."

Jane shook her head. "No. I saw Raul drag one back who was trying to escape, and then he had a guard hold her down while he raped her. Believe me; I saw more of him than I wanted to. Does he really think a tattoo of two pistols framing his dick is sexy?"

Bailey sat down on one of the chairs at her kitchen table. "I need to think," she whispered.

"There's no time. We need to leave," Cade said

unsympathetically.

"Please, Bailey, come with us. You know you can't stay here." She saw from the expression on Bailey's face that she didn't want to leave her husband, despite knowing he was a rapist. "Dad said, if you don't come back, he's going to stop your allowance. Do you think Raul is going to want you without that ten thousand placed in your checking account every month?"

Jane knew she had her there. Bailey shakily stood up, and they followed her to her bedroom where she began gathering her things.

"We can't take much," Cade warned her.

Bailey dropped the few items she had gathered onto her bed. "Let's go, then. You're not leaving me a choice either way."

Jane glared at her angrily before picking up a few of Bailey's clothes, thrusting them into a small overnight bag. Then they went back through the kitchen.

"Wait," Jane whispered, turning back to her sister.

"What?" Bailey asked.

"Do you have any candy bars?"

"Yes."

"Get them and any other food you can."

Bailey went to her cabinets. Several minutes later, she had placed a few items in a large cloth bag. She handed Jane the bag as they went out the door.

"You're worried about a candy bar? I know you're a food addict, but you're freaking crazy." Bailey threw her a scornful look which Jane ignored, holding the food items close to her chest.

"How are we going to get out of here?" Jane asked Cade, who was staring at both sisters contemptuously.

"I have a truck parked up ahead. I want to get as far away as we can before daylight."

"You two go ahead. Show me the direction you're headed, and I'll catch up," Jane told him.

"What? Where do you think you're going?" Cade

shifted his body closer to her.

"I'm going to release those women then catch up to you."

"No, you're not," Cade informed her. "There's no way you will be able to catch up to us."

"I will." Jane firmly took a step away from him. "I'm not leaving them behind. I'll catch up." She opened the palm of her hand, showing the key's to Raul's SUV that she had stolen from Bailey's kitchen counter. She had seen the vehicle parked in the driveway.

"Look, I feel bad for them, too. But it's either them or us." Cade tried to sway her, but self-preservation had never been her strongest personality trait.

She took another step back. "I won't leave them."

"Dammit to hell. You're going to get them and us killed."

"I think they would prefer death to what they're going through now," Jane said sadly. "I'm sorry. You two go."

"Fuck." Cade pointed to a palm tree. "Bailey, go hide over there. We'll be back in ten minutes."

"Wait, you can't leave me alone," she wailed.

"Go!" Cade ordered.

Her sister fled at the cold hostility in his voice.

"Let's do this." He moved off into the darkness, and she followed, carefully trying to be as quiet as he was.

He stopped not far from where the guard was once again positioned in front of the small house. Another soldier had appeared since they had left, probably changing shifts.

"Stay here," he ordered before stealthily moving closer to the men who weren't paying attention as they talked to each other.

A sharp sound of something thrown had both men turning, leaving Cade the perfect opening to jump them from behind. He stabbed one in the back, bringing him down, before struggling with the other one for his rifle. Using the rifle strap, he strangled the soldier.

Jane bit back her scream of protest, reason telling her it was either the guards or the women. It was a no-brainer.

Jane ran forward when Cade motioned for her after looking through the window. He hid the soldiers at the side of the house while Jane slowly opened the door.

The large room held five women who started to scream when they saw her enter, but Jane spoke to them softly in Spanish to make them understand she was there to help them.

"Does anyone understand that I'm here to help?" Jane asked hopelessly when they remained on their beds. She saw she wasn't getting through to them. They were too traumatized from their recent attack.

"I do." A woman with her face bruised and bloodied stood. Jane knew instantly it was the woman Raul had drug back.

"Great. Tell them I'm going to help them escape, but we have to be very quiet. I … I can't promise you we'll make it, so if they aren't sure, they should stay here."

The woman turned and quickly repeated her words in Spanish. Many of the women spoke up in agreement, and then the woman told Jane, "We all want to leave rather than stay with the monsters who have stolen us from our homes."

With that, Cade opened the door, motioning for them to exit. They filed from the room, following Cade through the night as he skirted the houses until they were back at Bailey's house.

Cade opened the door to Raul's SUV. "Get in."

The women climbed into the large vehicle with Jane helping those who had trouble. The one who had spoken up got behind the wheel when Cade asked who could drive.

"We're not going with them?" Jane asked.

"No. We have to split away from them." Cade, seeing her stubborn look, gave her an aggravated sigh. "It helps them, too. If they get caught with us, they'll immediately be killed. Instead, they'll probably be brought back here."

Neither scenario made Jane happy, but she nodded in understanding.

Going to the back window, she handed a woman the cloth-filled bag of food, keeping a couple of the candy bars for herself. Once the young woman gave her a timid smile, Jane moved away.

"Are you ready now?" he asked sarcastically.

"Yes."

"Then stay here while I go get our ride."

He turned to the woman who was going to drive. "As soon as I pull in behind you, drive in that direction." Cade pointed in the direction opposite from the one they would be going.

The woman nodded, gripping the wheel tightly.

Cade took off at a fast-paced jog. As soon as he was out of view, Jane saw headlights heading in their direction from the main house.

"Shit." What were they supposed to do now? She really became frightened when she saw it was two pairs of headlights.

Javier's men must have discovered they were missing.

Cade pulled up next to her from the opposite direction in a newer model truck than the last one he had borrowed.

He rolled the window down to yell, "Get in!"

Jane knew that, if they tried to run, they would be caught since there was a vehicle to follow each of them.

She reached in her pocket, pulling out the weapon she had found in the ammunition room, then took a step toward the cars that were almost on them. They were close enough that she could make out Raul's furious face.

Cade jumped out of the truck. "What are you doing?"

"Get Bailey." She hit the back window of the women's SUV. "Go!"

She pulled the pin, throwing it at Raul's car before running to the side of the truck, crouching down just before the explosion filled the air.

"What in the fuck did you just do?" Jane's ears were ringing from the deafening blast of the explosion, but she caught the drift of what Cade was saying as he dove for cover, barely missing being decapitated by a flying tire rim.

The SUV with the women took off with a wrenching of gears when several guards came running out of the second car. Fury blazed through Jane.

"Give me a minute," she told Cade, pulling out the other grenade. She looked at it quickly then pulled the pin.

"Have you lost your mind?" Cade yelled.

Jane threw the grenade toward the men who were running toward them, watching as the soldiers ran for cover. They were rocked off their feet, thrown back by the explosion. She didn't feel the least bit sorry for them as they lay in their own blood and body parts. Bailey had said the men respected violence; well, let them respect that a woman had beaten them at their own game.

"Okay, we can go now." She turned to look expectantly at Cade.

He waited for a second before coming out from behind the truck.

"Do you have any more?" he asked from between clenched teeth.

"No, that was it." Jane lied. The way he was looking at her was kind of scary.

"Bailey, move it!" Cade yelled, opening the truck door for her. Bailey ran forward from her hiding spot and climbed into the truck without stopping, and Jane jumped in behind her, sitting next to the door. Cade got behind the steering wheel, peeling out just as a disheveled, bloody Raul ran toward them.

"Bailey!" His scream had Bailey turning around to look out the back window.

"Let me out."

"No way. We're going home." Jane jerked Bailey back around, flipping her future ex-brother-in-law off.

Chapter Nine

"Where did you get those grenades?"

"I found them." Jane thought she heard his teeth grinding.

"You could have killed Raul!"

"I tried hard enough." Jane stared back at her sister, refusing to feel guilty. Those women deserved their freedom more than Raul deserved to be alive.

"Where are we going?" Jane asked a still angry Cade.

"To a friend of mine's house. He'll hide us for a couple of days until we can get out from the roads or have a plane flown in to meet us."

"How far away is it to your friend?"

"Not far. Still, not only will Javier's men be searching for us, but because of your stunt at the hotel, I had to ask around if anyone saw you, so Carlos has found out I'm in town, and his men are looking for me."

"So, we have two separate gangs trying to kill us?" Bailey squealed.

"Yes."

Jane had to bite back her smile, because it was obvious Cade had reached his limit with her and Bailey, and Bailey looked like she was about to cry over her lousy excuse of a husband. Jane was the only one taking everything in stride. Of course, she was the one causing them all the problems.

"What's so fucking funny?" Cade snarled.

"Life is looking pretty damn good right now."

While the cab filled with a strained silence, Jane leaned her head against the window and closed her eyes. She hadn't had very much sleep since she had left the States, and it was catching up with her. Her bones ached she was so tired, and she almost fell from her seat when Cade came to a sudden stop.

"What's wrong?" Jane tried to blink the sleep from her eyes.

"Nothing. We're here." Cade turned off the truck then stared at the house a few feet away.

"Then why aren't we getting out?" she asked, confused.

"I'm waiting for a signal," Cade answered, continuing to make no move to get out.

Jane looked at the house and saw a light suddenly come on in the front window.

"Everything's okay." Cade opened his truck door, stepping out.

Jane fumbled with the door handle, almost falling out, but Cade managed to catch her before she hit the ground.

"I didn't realize it was so high up," Jane mumbled, taking a step out of his arms.

Cade helped Bailey out before taking each of their arms to lead them to the house.

"Afraid your payday will get damaged?" Jane smarted off, instantly regretting it when his hand on her arm dropped away.

"I thought you may need some help." Cade's quiet

voice had Jane feeling ashamed of herself, especially when he paused and reached back inside the truck to pull her backpack out from behind the seat, handing it to her. She didn't know what it was about him that had her always snapping at him. Jane noticed he still maintained his grip on Bailey, who leaned farther into his side for support.

Cade knocked briefly on the door, and when no one answered, he opened the unlocked door then ushered them inside.

A tall, dark-haired man came in from what Jane assumed was the kitchen.

"Well, Cade, what trouble have you managed to get yourself into this time?"

* * *

Killyama parked her car in the parking lot of The Last Riders' clubhouse where several of the bikers were standing around talking. She glanced down at her watch. The factory where they put together and ship out survivalist gear would have closed for the night.

Pasting her usual scowl on her face, she climbed out of her old, puke green car, and the men stopped talking to stare in apprehension at her approach.

Razer, Viper, Cash, Shade, and Train all had the same look of horror on their faces. She wasn't put off by their attitudes, though. Hell, she relished it. She had cultivated it during the time she had known them.

"I need your help." Killyama didn't believe in beating around the bush.

"Why should we help you?" Train's smart-ass remark didn't surprise her. His wounded male pride was still stinging from her disappointment of his lackluster sexual performance. The dumb fuck couldn't believe she wasn't swooning to have another go-round on his dick.

"Because, if you don't, I'll ask Beth, Winter, and Lily for help." She watched their husbands' reactions to her threat.

"What do you want?" Viper snapped.

These men are pussy whipped and don't even know it, she thought caustically.

"Fat Louise has put herself in a fucked-up mess, and I need you to help me get her out."

"What kind of trouble?" Train asked suspiciously.

"She sneaked into Mexico to get her half-sister out."

The men stared at her blankly, completely surprised by her answer.

"Fat Louise? She doesn't even take a piss without one of you by her side," Razer commented. "Besides, why did she have to sneak? The federales want her?" he joked.

"You think this is funny?" she snapped, taking a step toward him.

"No." Razer didn't step back, but Killyama could tell he wanted to. She was satisfied with that little victory.

"Her dad is a government employee, doing some kind of secret shit for them. Employees and their family aren't allowed to travel in certain areas. He alerted Border Patrol, trying to stop her before she went inside, but he was too late."

"What in the fuck are we supposed to do?" Shade asked.

"You have connections. I need them to get me inside so I can find her."

"You're not going after her," Train stated angrily.

"Since when do you think you can tell me what I can do?" Killyama glared at him.

Train didn't back down. "Since you came up with a crazy-assed plan to try to enter a country that has made a career out of kidnapping and killing people," he snapped.

"Back off, lover boy. I'm going after her. Are you men going to help me or not?" She stressed the word men, letting them know it was an insult.

"Do we have a choice?" Viper asked snidely.

"No, but don't worry." She curled her lip. "I have a plan. Where's Dean?"

"Probably hiding if he saw you," Train said grimly.

"Get him. We're going to need him," Killyama ordered. "Knox, too. They will have the contacts we need to find Jane. Beth told us the strings he had to pull to find Lily when she went missing."

"Anything else?" Train asked sarcastically, pulling his phone out.

"Yeah, you can shove that phone up your ass when you're finished making those calls."

Train lowered the phone to his side, his face turning cold. As he took a step toward her, Killyama held her ground. It wasn't easy, and she found herself giving Razer extra kudos now that she was in his shoes. The easygoing Train she was familiar with had disappeared, and a man she hardly recognized stared back at her vengefully.

"We don't do jobs for free. If you want our help, you'll pay for it like everyone else."

"What's your price?" She placed her hands on her hips.

"I'll let you know when I decide."

"You're just going to hold it over my head until you decide?" she snapped.

"Yeah."

"I don't have a choice, do I?"

"No. Sucks, doesn't it?"

Killyama felt a chill race down her spine. She had blackmailed The Last Riders into helping her by using their wives, and Train had turned the tables on her by blackmailing her into doing something she was sure as fuck she wasn't going to like. For the first time, she felt a spark of attraction for the ladies' man of the club. She had never been attracted to pussies. Maybe there was hope for him yet.

Chapter Ten

The house was in ruins, its furniture broken and strewn around the small room.

"What are we going to do now?" Bailey snapped, glaring at her sister as if she was to blame for the house being destroyed. "It's not safe to stay here now."

Jane glared back at her ungrateful sister, wishing she could turn back time and reconsider her decision to rescue her. Her conscience came into play, though, remembering those women she had freed. If one had escaped, it had all been worthwhile.

"Be quiet," Cade ordered. "We'll stay here." He moved away, cautiously walking farther into the room and stepping over pieces of broken glass. "They've already searched here, so they have no reason to come back."

"That's what I'm thinking." The man held his hand out. "How you been, Cade?"

"Doing well, Felix. You?"

Felix kicked a broken lamp toward a stone wall. "I've been better."

Cade laughed. "I'll make it up to you for your trouble."

Felix stared at Bailey and Jane. "Pay's good?"

"I've had worse paying jobs," Cade acknowledged. "But I've had easier ones, too."

"Too much to handle?"

"One's a chore, two's a bitch." Jane had a feeling of which one he thought was the bitch.

Felix laughed. "You two hungry?"

"Yes," Jane admitted.

"How can you be hungry at a time like this?" Bailey turned an aggravated glance at her.

"Why shouldn't I be hungry? I wasn't the one who had to run away in the middle of the night from a husband who kidnaps and rapes women."

"See what I mean?" Cade broke into the budding argument.

"Si, Amigo. I will feed them then find some whiskey for us."

"I'd appreciate any help I can get."

Jane almost snapped at him, but then decided not to confirm that she was the bitch. Instead, she found a broom in the kitchen and began sweeping up as Felix fixed the food.

"You don't have to do that," Felix protested.

"I don't mind. I like keeping busy." Jane straightened the room as best she could, piling the smaller, broken pieces into the trashcan and making a pile of the larger pieces in the corner. Then she threw the destroyed couch cushions down on the floor for them to sit on.

Once Felix handed her and Bailey a plate with a sandwich and chips, both women sank to the cushions to eat their meal. Jane watched as Cade fixed his own sandwich, standing at the window to eat as he kept watch on the outside.

"I can't believe you stuck your nose in my business," Bailey complained in a low whisper. "You never could mind your own business, Fat Louise."

"Your mother is worried sick, and so is Dad. I couldn't watch them worry about you."

"Always eager to help. When are you going to learn that, unlike those loser friends of yours, I don't need your help?"

"My friends are not losers," Jane denied heatedly.

"Why don't you two shut the fuck up? Your big mouths are going to drive me nuts." Cade dropped a couple of blankets down next to where they were sitting before sitting on one. "Get some rest. We'll leave in a couple of hours. I want to get to our next stop before it gets dark again."

"A couple of hours?" Bailey asked, shocked.

"I don't want to take a chance on them coming back."

Bailey snapped her mouth closed, picking up a blanket for herself as she lay down. Jane curled her arms around her knees, leaning her forehead on them.

If Killyama were here, Bailey would be too afraid to mistreat me, Jane thought. *And Cade would be nicer to me. He would see I'm really not that bad.*

She missed her friends yet dreaded seeing them again. They were going to be furious with her for not telling them what she had planned.

She tried unsuccessfully to keep from sniffling, but Cade must have heard. He lowered the glass of whiskey Felix had given him.

"Come here."

Jane shuffled to his side, and Cade scooted over, giving her enough room to lie down.

"It's going to be all right," he said in a low voice.

"No, it's not. Javier or Carlos's men are going to catch us and kill us, my sister hates me for making her leave her husband, and if I do survive, my friends are going to kill me for doing this without telling them."

"We can make it to the border. This isn't the first time I've done this. And your sister is a bitch."

A loud snort came from Bailey at his words.

"And your friends will understand."

"If you think I'm a bitch, wait until you meet her friends," Bailey said snidely, rolling over to give them her back.

"Ignore her. Lie down and get some sleep."

Jane took his advice, lying down next to him. The night was chilly, and she shivered before moving closer to Cade. He gave an aggravated sigh and rolled to his side, pulling her toward him then placing an arm around her waist. Jane relaxed against him and closed her eyes. It was the first time she had felt safe since she left Jamestown.

Cade stared down at Jane in the morning light, fighting back the surge of protectiveness he felt for the woman. She wasn't what he had expected. He had anticipated a spoiled daddy's girl; instead, he had found there wasn't anything spoiled about her. She had been willing to sacrifice herself for those women being held captive, even giving them the only food they had. With no money, it hadn't been a smart move on her part. She hadn't known he planned to stop at Felix's for supplies, but she had kept the candy bars for herself. He thought about that with a wry smile. He had noticed when they had been stuck in the hotel for two days that she had a sweet tooth.

In her picture, she had been sitting on a couch that hadn't looked expensive, wearing jeans and a casual T-shirt, unlike the expensive dress her sister had worn. She shied away from any attention shown to her directly, probably the result of being overshadowed by her attention-seeking sister.

Her father was completely wrong about his daughters. Bailey was out for herself and would survive in shark-infested waters. Jane, on the other hand, would let the sharks have her if they were hungry.

Cade let the women sleep for a couple of hours,

keeping alert for anyone approaching the house. He woke them around noon, Bailey grumbling and Jane drowsily going to the restroom.

He fixed each of them a bowl of cereal and coffee.

"Eat up. We need to go." Cade pushed the bowl of cereal toward Bailey. Jane had already eaten half of hers.

"I don't eat food like this," Bailey complained.

"Right now, you can't be choosy. We can't exactly go in a store or restaurant, since there will most likely be a big reward posted for us. Anyone who catches sight of us could turn us in." He shoved the bowl back toward her. "Eat."

"I'll eat it if you still don't want it," Jane offered.

Cade saw Bailey throw her sister a dirty look before picking up her spoon. A slight smile was on Jane's lips as she finished her own. She had known how her sister would react. Bailey didn't want Jane to have anything of hers.

"How much longer before we leave? I'm ready to go home. If we are stopped at any road-blocks, I'll just tell them Raul is my husband. He can convince Javier to let you return to the States," Bailey said between bites of her food. "I don't know if he can help with Carlos, though. You might be on your own with him."

"Thanks." Cade really disliked this particular sister.

"You want to stay with him?" Jane's disgusted question raised her sister's fury.

"I shouldn't have left in the first place without talking to him. Maybe there was a reason—"

"There was a reason, but you just don't want to believe it," snapped Jane.

Bailey's lips tightened, and she grew quiet.

"I'm sorry, Bailey. I know you care about him, but I know what I saw."

The sound of laughter outside the house had Jane peeking outside. A young man was playing with a toddler across the street. There were more people out than when they had arrived during the night.

"I'll move your truck to the back of the house," Felix offered, and Cade tossed him the keys.

"Why can't we just drive to the airport and fly out?" Jane asked Cade the question that had been bothering her since they had arrived at the house.

"I wish I'd have thought of that. Maybe because Javier and Carlos would think of the same thing and post roadblocks," Cade replied caustically.

"There's no need to be rude. I was just wondering." Jane scooted her empty bowl away.

Cade felt guilty, and he didn't want to feel that way. He wanted to get rid of the women and get back to Martina. He promised himself a week in bed with her for the trouble this job had cost him. With the money he would make, he would be able to pay for it.

Jane went to stand at the window, watching the child who was now playing with his older brothers and sisters. The mother had come outside and was carefully watching over her children. Jane waved and began playing peek-a-boo with a child who was staring at her through the window, each of them laughing.

"You like children," Cade observed.

"My friend Sex Piston has a child that age. I also babysat her stepdaughter Star when she was younger."

Cade could tell from the affection in her voice that she missed her friends. He had heard her refer to them several times in the same tone; however, when she had talked about her parents, the affection was missing.

Cade and Jane were both still standing in the window when the dark cars pulled up. Cade pushed her back, moving the curtain back in place.

"Who is it?"

"Carlos. He already knows we're here." Felix hadn't returned with Cade's truck, making it obvious who had turned them in to Carlos.

"I'm sorry."

Cade turned to her in surprise.

"That your friend turned you in."

"Felix isn't a friend. I don't have friends. Felix just went for the bigger payday." Cade picked up the rifle he had brought in from the truck.

"Both of you go to the back door. When I tell you to run, fucking run like your lives depend on it. You understand me?"

Jane and Bailey nodded their heads. Jane tugged on her backpack as she went to the back door. Bailey stood by her sister, looking terrified.

Two men got out of each car, and Cade's nerves tautened when they told the parents and children to get inside. They were preparing for a battle.

Jane and Bailey waited for his signal. As soon as the door closed behind the small family, Cade placed the rifle in position before taking his shot. One of Carlos's men fell to the ground. Then Cade was able to bring down another one as the two edged closer to the door. Cade caught sight of one he hadn't seen try to go around back and cut off their escape.

"Run!" yelled Cade.

Both Jane and Bailey took off. When they did, the soldier moving toward the back took aim to fire at them, but Cade managed to shoot him.

The sound of more cars screeching to a stop clenched his balls. They weren't going to be able to fight off this many.

While the soldiers began filing out of the Jeeps, Cade managed to fire off another shot, wounding the last of the first four; however, he was trapped inside the house as the other soldiers ran forward. He was about to kiss his ass goodbye when he saw a flash of movement and an explosion sent the men flying in different directions. Cade looked in shock at Jane who was standing out in the open. She had thrown another fucking grenade.

If he lived through this, he was going to fucking check her pockets.

When, instead of running, she reached into her pocket again, the men took off, running for their lives.

Cade also used the opportunity to run, taking down a few more men who had decided it was safer to face a bullet coming in the front door than being outside with Jane.

"Let's go, Jane!" he yelled as he ran toward her, expecting to hear another explosion at any second.

He stopped when he saw Bailey struggling with one of Carlos's men. Putting his sights on the man, a child's cry had him turning. The parents had panicked and left their smallest child outside. Jane was running toward the child standing out in the open.

"Damn it to hell!"

A knife flashed as the soldier fighting Bailey decided he'd had enough of her struggles. Jane had a rifle pointed at her by another determined to bring her down. Cade only had a split second to make his decision on which one to save.

Pointing his rifle, he fired.

Chapter Eleven

"Stop!" The sharp order came from the man coming to a halt in a Jeep.

"Raul!" Bailey screamed as she stepped over the body of the man Cade had just killed.

Jane jumped for the small child, picking him up from the ground.

"Drop your weapon!" Raul ordered Cade.

Left with no choice, he dropped his rifle onto the ground as Jane handed the crying toddler to his father who had come running from their house.

"Raul!" As Bailey attempted to throw herself into his arms, the back of his hand sent her flying backward. Shocked, she held her hand to her face.

"You stupid whore." Raul took a step toward his wife, who backed away fearfully.

"Don't you dare!" Jane started to move toward her sister yet was held back by one of the soldiers.

Raul's cold eyes glared at her. "You're just as useless as your sister," he snarled. "If not for your father's money, I would never have touched her."

"Raul…" Bailey pleaded.

"Shut up with your whining. I've heard enough over the last few weeks." Raul turned from her and strode toward Cade, ordering, "Tie them up and put them in the cars"

As one of the soldiers struck Cade with the butt of his rifle, Jane winced, crying out. The soldier didn't hesitate as he threw her to the ground. One tried to take her backpack, and Jane attempted to jerk it away. She kept his attention focused on trying to tug the backpack away while she reached behind her back for the knife she had slipped into her jeans. Jerking hard on the strap, the soldier was slightly off balance, and Jane used his forward momentum to stab him, stepping to the side, before she tossed his gun to Cade.

Mayhem erupted.

"Run, Bailey!" Jane took off running toward an outcropping of rocks that weren't too far away. Bailey took one look at Raul's face and started fleeing.

"Don't shoot!" Raul's order shocked Jane, but she figured that, as hostages, they would be useless dead. Her father would demand proof of life before he would pay any ransom. Jane heard gunfire behind her yet didn't turn back to see how Cade was doing.

They managed to make it to the rock where they dropped down behind one to catch their breath.

"I hate you! This is all your fault!"

"Will … you … please … be quiet before they find us?" Jane said.

"I had a happy marriage before you showed up! You can fucking die for all I care." Bailey lowered her head to the rock and cried.

Jane belatedly realized her mistake. She should never have tried to save her ungrateful sister. She was with the sick son of a bitch she wanted. They deserved each other.

Jane crawled into the confined space. Peering over the

rocks, she saw the soldiers looking for them; however, Cade was nowhere to be seen.

Jane heard a sound to her left, tensing, and then gave a sigh of relief.

"Cade." He had blood dripping from a cut above his eye. "Are you all right?" she asked, afraid the soldiers would see her movements.

"No," he replied, grimacing as he hunkered down. His face was becoming a bloody mess.

"I'm sorry," Jane apologized.

"It's not your fault they found us," Cade reassured her. "You managed to save our asses."

"What are they going to do?"

"Search for us until they find us again," he answered truthfully, which Jane respected.

Bailey began wailing.

"Jesus, don't you ever shut up?" he snapped. "They'll kill me right away, but they're going to try to blackmail your father for money, so it will be awhile before they kill you two. Maybe he can secure your release. I don't know. It depends on if he can get the money to them."

"Maybe he won't have to," Jane uttered, scooting her body closer to his.

"What do you mean?" Cade asked her.

"We can walk out of Mexico. It's done all the time."

"I'm not walking." Bailey stuck her feet out, showing her shoes. The flat sandals would be no barrier to rocks and dirt.

Jane pulled off her tennis shoes, placing them next to Bailey. "Give me your sandals. I'll wear them." Bailey took off the sandals, putting on Jane's tennis shoes. Cade had hoped they wouldn't fit, but they did. Used to giving up her things to her spoiled sister, Jane had known they would.

"What now?" Bailey asked, tying the shoes.

"We'll wait and give the guards time to give up and search another area. Thank fuck it's so hot they won't search long."

"Come on." Cade told them as soon as the last of the Raul's men drove away and it became dark.

Jane and Bailey stood, beginning the long trek toward the border. Following Cade, they moved silently through the inky darkness. While they ran from the town through a wooded area, all Jane could hear was Bailey's complaining.

It didn't take long before Bailey bent over, crying out from a pain in her side.

"I can't run anymore!"

"If you don't be quiet, I'm going to strangle you," Cade threatened.

Bending over, he tossed her over his shoulder and kept running. Jane ignored her own exhaustion, trying to keep up as best she could.

She didn't know how long they ran before they stopped to rest. Jane was relieved, uncertain how much farther she could have gone.

"We'll rest here for a few minutes then leave. We need to get as far as we can while it's dark.

Jane took a drink from the bottled water she had in her backpack. Thank God she had been smart enough to pick it up before running away from the soldier she had stabbed. She then passed it to Bailey who took deep gulps of the precious liquid.

"Don't drink it all," Cade said, taking the water away.

"I'm still thirsty," she complained.

"This water may have to last us awhile." He took a small sip for himself before closing it.

"That's not enough," Jane protested.

"It's enough for now." He got back to his feet. "Let's get going."

This time, Bailey walked. She was slower, but at least she was carrying her own weight.

It was still dark when they found an abandoned RV riddled with bullet holes next to a small pond.

"Am I dreaming?" Jane asked as Cade cautiously

scouted out the deserted area.

"No. It must have belonged to someone transporting illegals or drugs. They used it because of the water"—he pointed to the pond—"and it's secluded. We should be able to hide out here for the day. It doesn't look like anyone's been here for a while."

Jane investigated the RV. It had been ransacked, with nothing left behind. There was a thin mattress lying on the floor. Jane was forgetting what it was like to sleep in a normal bed.

She turned the mattress over, seeing it looked somewhat cleaner on that side.

"Go ahead and lie down, Bailey."

Her sister lay down without offering her thanks. She didn't even move over so Jane could lie down, even though there was room. Jane's shoulders sank as she turned away, laying down her backpack on the floor and using it as a pillow.

When Cade returned, he paused in the doorway, taking in the difference in the girls' positions. Jane saw his lips tighten.

"Come lie next to me," Bailey offered Cade the spot next to her.

"Jane, go lie down with your sister. I'll take the floor."

As Jane got off the floor and went to lie uncomfortably next to her sister while Cade lay on the floor, she felt Bailey's anger through the darkness. Jane didn't have time to wonder at her sister's behavior, though. She was too tired. She fell asleep, clinging to the side of the mattress to give Bailey more room.

* * *

Bright sunlight woke her. Jane's aching fingers released her grip on the mattress. As she looked around the small trailer, she saw she was alone. Jane was frightened until she heard her sister's voice from outside. Stiffly, she climbed off the mattress and went to the door of the trailer.

Cade and Bailey were sitting next to each other by the

pond talking. Jane had seen that look on women's faces too many times not to know what it meant. Her sister was attracted to Cade. She was looking up at him beneath lowered lashes, smiling at him flirtatiously.

Jane felt her stomach sink. Her sister always managed to snare any man she wanted, and now she had definitely picked Cade as her replacement for Raul now that she realized the chances of them getting back together were nil.

Jane walked forward, hearing them talk about Bailey's visit to Europe.

"You'll have to visit when we get out of here," she was saying.

"I'll think about it," Cade answered noncommittally.

"I thought we would have left by now," Jane interrupted.

Cade shrugged. "If we move out in the open, they'll see us for sure. If we wait here, we can leave when it gets dark. We're close enough to the boarder to make a run for it if we hear any vehicles approaching."

Bailey jumped to her feet. "Do you think it would be possible to take a quick dip if I hurry? I feel filthy in these clothes."

"Go ahead. I'll keep an eye out. Just don't take long." Cade stood up, brushing the dirt off his pants.

Jane was shocked at her sister's behavior when she didn't wait for Cade to turn his back before she started stripping off her clothes. She wanted to smack her sister as she waded in naked, taking her time before lowering her body into the water.

Cade made no pretense of not watching, and Jane couldn't blame him. Her sister had large breasts and a small waist that flared out to curvy hips. She had shaved her pussy, which highlighted her long, golden legs. Bailey had not had anything to do for the last few weeks except sunbathe while her family worried about her.

Cade's amused expression caught hers. "Don't you

want to clean up?"

Jane's hand went to her dirt smeared face. "No, thanks." She sat down on the bank of the pond, averting her eyes as her sister made the most of the male attention she was receiving.

Jane's eyes widened when her sister came out of the water, taking her time to get redressed.

"Do you have a comb, Jane?"

"No."

Bailey gave a fake laugh. "You have grenades but no comb?"

"No, I don't," Jane repeated. "Maybe you can find something inside. I didn't look in the overhead cabinets."

Bailey went in the trailer to look.

"You and your sister don't get along, do you?" Cade asked, not taking his attention from the area surrounding them.

"No. We didn't grow up together, but I hear a lot of sisters don't get along." Jane tried to make light of the situation. She had tried to be close to Bailey, yet Bailey had rebuffed all of Jane's attempts.

"She try to steal all your boyfriends?" Cade teased.

"There weren't any to steal," Jane confessed. "She doesn't care for any of my friends."

"You haven't had any boyfriends, but you have male friends?"

"I have a lot of those. I belong to a motorcycle club. At least, I think I belong. My friend Sex Piston does. Her father was the former president and her husband is now. Since I'm her friend, it means I'm a member, too, doesn't it?"

Cade just stared at her. "You don't know?"

Jane bit her lip. "Of course I know. I am a member." She nodded her head, trying to convince herself. "Stud, let's all of us hang out at the clubhouse."

"Who's Stud?"

"Sex Piston's husband. He's a nice guy. Me and my

friends really like him."

"They all have nicknames like Stud and Sex Piston?"

"Of course," Jane stated. "There's also Killyama, Crazy Bitch, and T.A. We've all been friends since grade school, except Sex Piston. She didn't join our group until middle school."

"What's your nickname?"

"Fat Louise."

He stopped looking around, turning to study her, instead. "Fat Louise?"

"I was a little chunky when I was younger," Jane admitted.

Cade stared at her doubtfully.

"It's true." She nodded. "I have to work hard to keep the weight off. I like to eat a lot."

"You look like you need to gain ten pounds."

Jane shook her head. "No, I'm exactly the weight I'm supposed to be, according to my height and age."

"How do you know that?"

"Because I work to stay in that range."

"Does it really matter if you're a few pounds above?"

"Yes," Jane said grimly. She had worked hard to lose the weight.

"Bailey doesn't seem to be having any trouble with her weight," Cade remarked.

"No, she doesn't." She lowered her lashes to hide her hurt reaction at him comparing the two of them.

"What I meant was that maybe, if you weren't as active when you were younger, you might not need to watch your diet as closely now that you're older."

"Did you miss the part where I said I like to eat a lot?"

Cade's mouth curled in a smile, the first genuine one she had seen since she met him. She felt her nipples tighten. Embarrassed by her reaction, she glanced shyly away. If one of her friends was nearby, she would have felt more comfortable, maybe even casually flirted with him, but she didn't have any confidence without them.

"Was my father very upset?" Jane asked, changing the subject.

"Your father seems the type to think no problem can't be solved with his money."

"Unfortunately, that's true. He thought getting Raul to sign that prenup he had drawn up would protect Bailey. I tried to tell him not to keep giving Bailey such a high allowance after they married, but he wouldn't listen. I think, without the money, he wouldn't have brought Bailey with him."

"I don't, either. He seems like a dick. I can see why no one in the family likes him." He rubbed the badly bruised side of his face.

"Would you like me to clean up your face for you? It's in pretty bad shape."

Cade stared at her in amusement. "Have at it."

Jane dug into her backpack, pulling out a shirt. Ripping off a section that seemed fairly clean, she used the water in the canteen to wet it. Then she dug in her pack again for some salve she had put in before coming into Mexico.

"You got a first aid kit in there, as well?"

"No." Jane laughed. "Just Neosporin. I'm kind of a pack rat."

She motioned for him to sit down and then carefully scrubbed his face of the dried blood, trying not to hurt him. She felt a blush rise in her cheeks as he stared up at her.

After she finished cleaning him off, she dabbed the salve onto the cuts. Putting the cap back on, she took a step backward, forgetting her backpack was behind her. She started to fall, but Cade's hands reached out to steady her. She balanced herself by placing her hands on his shoulders.

"I'm a little clumsy," she said, beginning to straighten.

His hand left her waist to slide to the nape of her neck, holding her in place. Surprised, she froze as he brought his mouth closer to hers. Jane lowered her eyes to his mouth, waiting for his kiss.

"What's going on?" Bailey asked, stepping out of the trailer while running a brush through her hair.

"Nothing. I was just patching up Cade's face."

Bailey didn't look happy. "I should have offered. Are you okay?" she crooned, coming up behind him to place a comforting hand on his back.

Jane turned and picked her backpack up before going back into the trailer. I wanted that freaking kiss, Jane thought, mourning the loss of a second kiss from him, one where he wouldn't be pretending. She didn't stand a chance against her sister's more obvious flirtation, though.

She sat down on the mattress, wishing Killyama was there to kick Bailey's ass for her. The longer she sat there fuming, the angrier she got. Why should she let her sister keep her from trying to get to know Cade better? She might not be as pretty as Bailey, but she sure as shit had a better personality.

Standing up, she decided to make her own play for Cade instead of running like a wimp and leaving the field wide open for Bailey.

She came to an abrupt stop in the doorway.

Cade and Bailey were plastered together, with him giving her the same passionate kiss he had once given to Jane, except the one he was giving Bailey looked real.

Chapter Twelve

They began walking again as the sun set, with Jane behind Bailey, whose energy seemed restored. She kept a constant stream of chatter going until Cade was forced to quiet her, telling her the sound of voices would travel in the night. Thankfully, his reprimand managed to quiet her, and Jane was given a respite. She made sure to keep space between her and Cade as they traveled through the night. Cade shot her several curious looks yet didn't question the distance she had placed between them.

When they stopped to rest, Bailey sat down next to him, leaning against him as if they were already a couple, talking to him in low whispers that had Jane feeling like a third wheel.

She rose to her feet, turning to walk a few feet away.

"Where are you going?" .Cade's hand on her arm stopped her.

"I need to find a place to use the restroom," she told him softly.

"Hurry." Cade released her arm.

Jane hurried a few more feet away until she felt comfortable enough to lower her pants and relieve herself. When she came back to the camp, Cade was still sitting next to Bailey, her hand lying intimately on his thigh.

"How much longer before we get to the border?" Jane asked as she found a place to sit down until they started walking again.

"If we can walk some tomorrow without getting caught, we should make it tomorrow night."

Jane felt relief flooding her. She didn't know how much longer she could watch Bailey throw herself at Cade. She forced the feelings of jealousy away. She had never envied Bailey anything—not her father or the attention she managed to get from all their family members, and certainly not the boyfriends she had gone through over the years. However, Jane was finding it hard not to feel envious of the escalating intimacy growing between the two.

"Ready?" Cade and Bailey had risen to their feet and were waiting on her.

"I'm coming." Jane found herself following behind once more, gritting her teeth when Bailey began talking again. This time, she kept her voice to a low whisper so Cade couldn't reprimand her.

In the morning, they weren't lucky enough to find another RV, although they did find a small crevice in the side of a hill they could hide in.

"I'm starving," Bailey complained.

Jane sat down, hugging her knees, feeling her sister's glare on her as she complained. She tugged her backpack closer and unzipped it to take out the last candy bar. Tearing it in half, she gave a piece to Bailey, and then tore the other part in half again, giving that piece to Cade.

"No thanks, I'm good. You eat it." While Cade gave

her a hard stare, refusing to take it, Jane returned the stare, continuing to hold the candy out until Cade gave in, taking it from her.

"We don't have too much farther to go. We'll be crossing the border at Hidalgo, Texas, but it won't be safe to stay there, since the same criminals do business on both sides of the border. When we get to Corpus, I'll buy you both a steak," Cade promised, taking a seat closer to the opening.

"Let me have your backpack, Jane." Bailey rudely held out her hand.

Jane lifted her head. "Why?"

"I want to use it as a pillow," she snapped, taking it without so much as a thanks when Jane handed it to her.

Cade frowned, opening his mouth then closing it, and Jane wondered what he had been about to say.

While she tried to make herself as comfortable as possible, Cade straightened out his legs. Reaching out, he curled his hand around the nape of her neck and pulled her down until her head rested on his thighs. She lay stiffly, unable to relax with Bailey's eyes spitting fire. Jane closed her own to shut her anger out. Cade's comforting hand didn't move away; instead, he gently stroked her neck until she fell asleep.

It seemed like only a few minutes before she was being shaken awake.

"Is it time to leave already?" she asked drowsily.

"Yes, I want to get started," Cade answered.

They crawled out of the crevice.

"What time is it?" Jane asked, staring at the large expanse of land around them.

"Around noon."

They walked for a while before Jane realized she had left her backpack behind.

"Forget it. We don't need it," Bailey said.

Jane looked at Cade in question. "It's too far to go back for it now. Hopefully, we won't need it."

Jane nodded unhappily. There wasn't much left in the bag. Besides, the contents weren't important to anyone other than her, although it was handy to have when she wanted to stash something.

"We're getting closer to the border. They'll probably have people stationed at a few of the crossing, watching for us," Cade warned.

They passed several small villages on their way. The curious looks from the town people heightened Jane's fears that they would be stopped.

Bailey quieted, the tension finally succeeding in silencing her.

"Let's stop here while we still have a little cover. As soon as the sun goes down, we're going to reach the border," Cade informed, telling both women without words that they were entering dangerous territory.

Jane nervously ran her hands along the sides of her pants.

"You don't think Raul would really hurt us, do you?" Bailey asked when Cade went to scout ahead.

Jane remained silent, not wanting to lie.

"Why would he hurt us when he can get money out of Dad?"

Jane couldn't keep the contempt out of her eyes at Bailey's unconcern for their father being extorted by her husband.

"Don't look at me that way!" sneered Bailey. "You're no goody two shoes. You hang out with bikers and trash."

"Don't talk about my friends that way," Jane warned in a low voice.

"It's true. Hell, you're nothing but their little ass kisser. Anytime they need something done that none of them want to do, they just get you to do it."

"It's not true, and you know it for a fact." Jane leaned forward so Bailey couldn't mistake her meaning. "You don't like them because they know you're a fucking bitch. You're afraid of Sex Piston, Killyama, T.A., and Crazy

Bitch."

"I am not."

"Yes, you are, and we both know why." Jane had dealt with enough.

Standing up, she walked away to put a few feet between her and her sister. She walked farther than she realized and stared around in dismay, not seeing Bailey or Cade. She spun in a circle, not spotting anything she recognized, and began to panic. She was totally confused as to which direction she had come from.

While her instincts screamed at her to keep moving, calm reasoning kicked in, and she stood still, hoping the soldiers didn't find her before Cade.

She didn't see him until he was almost on her.

"What in the fuck is wrong with you?"

"I'm sorry. I got lost."

His hands reached out, grabbing her arms. "You're lucky I don't pull those pants down and smack that ass."

"I'm sorry," she repeated with tears brimming in her eyes.

"Stop crying!" Cade said heartlessly. His face was a mask of harsh recrimination. "Are you trying to get us all killed? Were you trying to get my attention?"

"No!" Jane was aghast at his interpretation of what had happened.

"Well, you have all my attention now, so what are you going to do with it?" he went on, ignoring her denial.

"What?"

Cade jerked her to his chest, his mouth cruelly covering her trembling one. She tried to turn her head, but his hand went to her jaw, holding her in place.

"You wanted to kiss me again, didn't you?" he gibed.

He covered her mouth again before she could deny his accusation, trying to part her lips with his tongue. Jane refused to let him deepen the kiss, but Cade wasn't a man who took denial easily.

"Open your mouth."

Jane tightened her lips, giving a whimper as his knuckles brushed against her nipples. With a gasp of shock, her lips finally parted, and his tongue claimed her mouth, discovering the sweet interior without caring, seeking to humiliate her. Jane managed to put her hands on his chest, thrusting herself away from him.

"You bastard."

"That's right. I am. And I'm fed up with you two. Both of you need to quit worrying about who's going to get inside my pants instead of getting our asses out of here alive!"

"Bailey can have your damn dick. I don't want it."

"Oh, you want it, Jane. Don't lie." His eyes traveled insultingly over her body. "I don't even mind taking both of you up on your invitations, but you'll have to wait until we're in a hotel where I don't have to worry about being sneaked up on by drug runners while taking a piece of pussy."

Jane could only look at him with wounded eyes at his sarcasm. She refused to deny his accusations any further.

"Which way back?"

When Cade pointed to the direction over her shoulder with a mocking twist to his lips, Jane pivoted on her blistered feet and began walking. She didn't say a word to him, dismayed at how long it took her to walk back to a furious Bailey who was waiting for her return.

"Could you be any more childish?"

"Forget it. Let's get going," Cade interrupted Bailey's coming storm.

The three took off. Jane was already tired from her impetuous walk, and Cade hadn't given her time to rest. He pushed them toward the border with no consideration that both women were tired and hungry.

"Fuck." As Cade came to a stop, Jane barreled into him from behind.

"What?" she asked, trying to look over his shoulder.

"We have a welcoming committee."

Chapter Thirteen

The three of them stared at the mass of people trying to get through the border. Well before that were several men in Jeeps who were looking through the crowds as they passed.

"They're searching for us," Jane stated.

"No shit." Cade ran a hand through his hair.

"What are we going to do?" Bailey questioned.

"Won't the soldiers on the other side help?" Jane asked.

"No." His answer dashed any hope she had that there would be an intervention to save their lives. "We're going to have to find a place in town where we can stay until we can—"

"I want to go home," Bailey whined. "I didn't want to be here in the first place. If the soldiers see us trying to get through, they'll help. They won't watch us die."

"Yes, they will," Cade told her. "It's not safe for us to stay in Reynosa."

Jane knew she was in trouble from his words, beginning to feel sick. She tried to think of what to do next when Bailey took off running, finally having reached her breaking point at Cade's words.

"Bailey!" Jane yelled, trying to stop her, which wasn't the smartest move.

One of the soldiers pointed in their direction as Jane ran after Bailey, trying to catch her, but the woman had received a burst of energy from God knew where and was covering the ground with remarkable speed.

Cade ran past her, taking Jane's hand. "It's too late. They've spotted us. We have to make a run for it."

While Cade pulled her along after him, she almost tripped and fell several times. If he hadn't been holding her hand, she would have.

The soldiers had just started their Jeeps, intending to cut them off, when Jane heard a shout. At first she thought it was Bailey yet then realized the sound was coming from the edge of the crowd.

A woman separated herself from a large group that had entered Mexico.

"Killyama!" Jane screamed in excitement and terror that her friend had just placed herself in danger. Three men came to flank Killyama as they all ran toward Jane, Cade, and Bailey. The soldiers were going to reach them first, though.

They all pointed their guns at them, and Jane waited for the pain of the bullets to hit her. Instead, what she felt was a sudden gust of wind that nearly sent her flying. A large helicopter appeared, dropping down to block the Jeeps.

"Get in!" yelled Rider.

Shots rang out as the soldiers began firing at the helicopter. Guns appeared from the inside, and the enemy fire was returned with deadly accuracy.

After Bailey threw herself into the helicopter, Jane felt

herself lifted by Cade and flung inside with his body covering hers.

Jane stared as Rider, Viper, and Shade shot rifles out of the opening of the helicopter. She felt others climbing in then recognized Killyama's voice.

"Go! Go!"

The helicopter lifted off with Train at the controls and Cash next to him.

Cade didn't lift his body off hers until the sounds of bullets were a distance away. As soon as his body moved to the side, she found her friend staring at her grimly.

Jane threw herself into Killyama's arms, bursting into relieved tears. All the terror she had suppressed since she had made the decision to save Bailey was now released in the safety of her friend's arms.

Killyama's arms tightened around Jane. Her usually frigid demeanor didn't soften as she held her, but her tight hug showed she cared.

"I'm going to beat the shit out of you for this. You know that, don't you?" Her harsh statement wasn't effectively delivered with the choked voice she tried to clear.

Jane nodded against her shoulder. "I deserve it," Jane hiccupped, trying to gather her control, feeling silly with The Last Riders and Cade silently watching.

Killyama pushed her back a few inches, staring into her eyes. "You okay?" She reached into her pocket, pulling out a protein bar and handing it to her.

"I am now." Jane grinned back.

"Sex Piston is going to be furious when she sees your hair."

Jane self-consciously brushed her hair back from her face that was dirty and probably sticking out in all directions. "She can fix it."

Her eyes went to Cade and Killyama's followed.

"He the one your dad sent in after you?" she asked.

"Yes."

"He wasn't doing a great job, was he?" she sneered.

Cade stiffened. "I was doing fine until Bailey took off like a bat out of hell."

Bailey flushed yet defended herself. "It worked out fine, didn't it? We're all safe now."

"No thanks to you," snorted Killyama.

Bailey threw her a dirty look, which Killyama returned with one of her own.

It was twenty minutes later before they set the helicopter down on the roof of a hotel.

"Everybody out. I have to get this baby back before someone notices it missing," Train yelled over the loud noise.

Cade jumped out first to help the women out. Bailey took her time, clinging to Cade much longer than necessary. Next was Jane, who felt a spark of electricity as his hands circled her waist when he lifted her to the ground. Killyama moved next to her, not wanting help to exit.

"Killyama!" Jane and her friend both turned around at Train's yell.

"Remember our deal. I'll be calling it in soon."

"Deal with this!" Killyama shouted above the roar of the blades, making an obscene gesture before jumping out of the helicopter.

Jane noticed the wary look on her friend's face as they waited for the helicopter to take off with The Last Riders inside.

"How did you get them to help?" Jane asked, watching them fly away, no doubt heading straight home to Kentucky as soon as they dropped off the helicopter.

"You don't want to know. Put it this way, you owe me one, bitch."

"I already knew that." Jane smiled at her friend.

The four went down a flight of stairs before finding an elevator.

"Your dad is here. He's booked several rooms for us to

stay in until we can get a flight out."

The elevator reached their floor, and Killyama led them to a suite. When the door opened, Bailey broke away from them, running to their father who stood up from a chair.

"Bailey!" Her father embraced Bailey with tears in his eyes. "My baby."

Jane stood by, feeling like a third wheel. After several minutes, he turned with his arm around Bailey.

"Jane." He held out his free arm to her. Jane stepped forward, letting her father embrace her for a moment before stepping away.

"Are you two all right?" he asked, gazing down at Bailey.

"I'm fine. Jane is, too," Bailey answered. "What I need is some food and something cold to drink."

He laughed. "I'll order it now. What would you like?"

Bailey gave her father a large order, which he relayed to room service.

"Jane?"

"Anything is fine, but I'll take a hamburger if they have it."

"Cade?"

"I'll grab something later. What I want is a shower and a bed."

"Of course." Her father finished their order before hanging up the phone, and then he went to a side table, handing Cade a card key to his own room. "Thanks, Cade."

Cade nodded before turning to leave without saying a word of goodbye.

Jane swallowed back the lump in her throat.

"Wait, Cade. Don't forget you promised me dinner when we got back," Bailey stopped him.

"I remember. I'll meet you downstairs tonight at eight," he said, going out the door.

She felt the silent scrutiny of Killyama as Bailey gave a bright smile to their father.

"I think I'll grab a quick shower while we wait for the food," Jane said, wanting to escape from her friend's watchful gaze.

"Certainly." Her father pointed to a doorway. "You can take that one. Bailey, the one next to it."

The women separated. Jane went into the bedroom, aware that Killyama was following on her heels.

"I packed you a bag," Killyama said, throwing herself down on the bed.

"Thanks for everything." Jane shut the bedroom door.

"You're welcome, but you're still not out of trouble with me."

"I know." Jane grimaced in dread as she opened the suitcase. She pulled out a pair of jeans, a T-shirt, and knee-high, black leather boots. Killyama had picked the clothes she usually wore around her friends, not the more conservative ones she wore around her father and work.

She showered then changed as Killyama took her turn in the shower.

As Killyama was getting dressed, she stared at her intently.

"What?" Jane asked.

"Nothing." Her friend shrugged, putting on her boots. "Cade's a good-looking man."

"Yes, he is," Jane acknowledged.

"You fuck him?"

Her bluntness didn't startle Jane. "No, he's a mean person." Jane licked her dry lips. "Besides, Bailey has her eyes on him."

"So what?"

"You know what Bailey's like when she wants something."

"She been up to her old tricks?"

"No, she's too scared of you and the rest of the girls to be too nasty to me."

Killyama relaxed her fighting stance. "So, what's the problem, then? You have the same equipment she has."

"I haven't decided if I want him yet."

"Well, you better make your mind up," she said matter-of-factly. "We're going home tomorrow, and I'm willing to bet Bailey won't be sitting around, trying to make up her mind."

"I'll think fast." Jane grinned.

"Think about what? Fuck him then make up your mind. He might fuck like a steer instead of a bull," Killyama warned.

Jane laughed. "Is that what happened between you and Train?"

Killyama gave a wicked grin. "Hell no. I thought I had myself a steer; instead, I had a mother fuckin' bull."

Chapter Fourteen

The meal with her father and Bailey was a disaster. She blamed their father for overreacting about Raul, telling him she had been perfectly safe, that it was only when Jane had shown up that the situation had become dangerous.

Jane didn't try to defend herself, though she did roll her eyes several times. Jane had, however, reminded Bailey that she had witnessed Raul raping a woman and that the mark on her face was from him slapping her.

"It was an extenuating circumstance," she said, brushing over the incident of her abuse, not mentioning the attack on the other woman.

Her father sat in his chair, listening. "Well, thank God it's over. I'll call a lawyer first thing in the morning to see about getting the divorce started. You need to change the information on your accounts and block Raul from trying to get his hands on your money."

"I'll take care of it," Bailey promised.

"Immediately," their father told her with a hard glint in his eyes which Jane had never seen before when he was talking to his youngest daughter.

"I said I would," Bailey soothed in the little girl voice she always used to twist him around her little finger. Predictably, her father was pacified.

Bailey placed her napkin on the table, standing up. "I'm going to take a nap before I meet Cade for dinner."

"Both of us are meeting him for dinner," Jane told her firmly. "He offered to take both of us out."

Bailey gave a quick nod, belaying the angry glare she wanted to throw across the room at her.

"Cade isn't the type of man either one of you should be having dinner with."

Her father's reaction startled her.

"I thought you knew him…"

He shook his head. "I never met him before I hired him to bring you two home. He has a dangerous reputation with his enemies and women, Jane."

"I wasn't planning on a serious relationship. It's just dinner."

"For you. I'm not so sure about Bailey. You know how she is. She has to have someone waiting when she goes through a break up."

Bailey took after her father in that respect, while she took after her mother in going after what she wanted.

"I wouldn't worry. He said he was leaving tomorrow. What could happen in one night?"

* * *

Jane started to get dressed as the time grew closer to meet Cade. She didn't have much of a choice with the limited clothes Killyama had brought her.

"Jesus, pick something already." Killyama was lying across her bed, reading a magazine.

"I don't know what to wear," Jane confessed, certain her stepmother would have packed Bailey's suitcase with several outfits.

Killyama raised her hand, searching carelessly through the clothes until she found a deep purple mini-dress. "Wear that." She plopped back down on the bed, turning another page in her magazine.

Jane put it on, realizing she didn't have any shoes to wear with the sexy dress.

Killyama gave an aggravated sigh, closing her magazine before going to her own suitcase to pull out a pair of high heeled boots.

"You ready for me to do your hair?"

"Please."

Jane sat down on the bench in front of the bed. Killyama climbed off, grabbing the brush and hairspray she never left home without. She went to work on the short locks, teasing and spraying Jane's fine hair to give it volume. When she was done, she lightly applied some make-up yet accentuated her eyelids with a darker color.

"There." Killyama took a step back, admiring her handiwork. "You look sexy as shit. That bitchy sister of yours doesn't stand a chance."

"You think so?" Jane asked, staring at herself in the mirror.

"Fuck, yeah. You better go. Don't give her too much time alone with the dude."

Jane jumped up, giving her friend a hug. "I love you. You're the best."

"Don't I know it?" She collapsed back onto the bed. "Have fun, girl. Wake me in the morning to tell me how he was."

Jane left the room laughing. She went to Bailey's door, knocking on it softly.

Her father opened his bedroom door.

"She left an hour ago. I thought you went with her," he said, surprise on his face.

"I must have misunderstood the time." Jane hadn't misunderstood. Bailey was pulling a fast one.

She told her dad goodnight before leaving.

She would go downstairs. They should still be eating. She was determined to at least have an hour of Cade's company, if nothing else than to tell him goodbye and thank him for his help. She told herself that over and over to build up her courage as she went downstairs.

When she entered the restaurant, however, she couldn't find them. Bailey must have talked him into taking her somewhere else to eat. She wasn't going to leave the hotel to search for them, though. Disheartened, she decided to return to the hotel suite.

She stepped out of the elevator, walking toward her room, when a door at the end of the hall opened and her sister came out, still straightening her clothes.

"I'll be back in a few. I'm just going to grab my suitcase," she said before closing the door.

Jane froze as Bailey sauntered down the hallway with a triumphant smile on her face.

"I'm spending the night with him," she gloated as she drew near.

"So I heard," Jane replied as she opened the door to their suite.

Bailey closed the door behind them. "You don't have anything to say?"

"Have fun," Jane told her, walking toward her room.

Her hand was on the doorknob when Bailey said, "Don't be such a spoilsport, Jane. He's too much for you to handle, anyway; believe me." She gave a tiny shiver of remembered pleasure, rubbing salt into the wounds.

"You're right; he is." Jane turned the knob, opening the door, but another one of her sister's wisecracks stopped her.

"You can have him when I'm done."

Jane turned around, her eyes frosting over. "I don't want him. I was going to thank him for helping us, but I shouldn't have bothered. Dad's money is thanks enough. Enjoy your relationship while it lasts, Bailey. I'm done."

"What do you mean?" Her sister lost her gloating demeanor.

"It means I'm done saving you. No more rescue trips to foreign countries, no more late nights where I have to bail you out of jail, no more giving you most of my allowance because you overspent yours, no more anything, Bailey. I'm done with you." Jane went into her room, closing the door behind her.

Killyama was standing in the middle of the room with a furious expression on her face. "I'm going to beat the shit out of her."

"Leave it alone. I'm glad I'm finally free of her. What time does our plane leave tomorrow?"

"Not until four. It's your dad's private jet."

"You think you can get us out of here tonight?" Jane pleaded.

"What do you think? Don't I always come through for you?"

Yes, you do, Jane acknowledged silently.

Killyama, Sex Piston, T.A., and Crazy Bitch were her sisters. They were all she was ever going to need.

Chapter Fifteen

"What bug crawled up your ass?" Sex Piston slid a basket of Popeye's chicken across the table.

"I'm not hungry." Jane slid the basket of food back.

"Shit, I'll eat them." Crazy Bitch snagged the basket with a long, manicured fingernail, dragging it toward her.

"You've been acting depressed since you came back a month ago. Did something happen while you were gone that you didn't tell us about?" Sex Piston's sharp gaze narrowed on her.

"No."

"It's what didn't happen that has her so upset," Killyama informed their friends. "She wanted to get laid, but her sister beat her to the dude."

"Then forget him," Crazy Bitch advised.

It isn't that easy, Jane thought to herself. She had tried not to think about him, but he always ended up on her mind somehow. She kept picturing his dark eyes and dark hair and how he had kissed her. She couldn't explain her reaction to the man whose attitude screamed loner. Hell, he hadn't even been nice to her. The part that drew her to him was that he came across as rude and uncaring yet had done little things like calm her fears or let her lay on his legs when it had to be uncomfortable.

Jane had learned long ago that truly mean people didn't do small kindnesses. In a way, his attitude reminded her of Killyama, who tried to come off as a mean-spirited woman, but underneath, she was protective and loyal.

"I have," she lied.

None of her friends believed her.

"You haven't wanted to go out since you came back." Sex Piston slapped her hand down on the table. "Tonight, you're going to the club. One of the brothers will take your mind off that fuck-bag."

"I can't tonight. I'm going to my dad's house to help him pack. He's moving back to New York since he decided to get a divorce."

"What does him getting a divorce have to do with New York?" T.A. asked.

"Bailey doesn't want to live here, so to make her happy, he's moving back." Jane was well aware that she would always come second in her father's eyes.

"I'm surprised she stayed here as long as she has," Crazy Bitch remarked.

"Dad's been looking for a new property to buy. He closed on it yesterday."

"Why doesn't she help Daddy pack?" Sex Piston said snidely.

"Her divorce has run into a snag with Raul still in Mexico, and she's upset."

"I haven't noticed it keeping her from fucking every man who catches her eye," Sex Piston told them. "I saw her with Kevin Parker, and she was all over him. His wife should beat the shit out of her. Then Stud and I were coming out of the grocery store with the kids when we ran into Bailey. The bitch flirted with Stud like I wasn't even there."

"What did you do?" Killyama laughed.

"Told her I would kick her skanky ass back to Mexico if she talked to Stud again," she said vengefully.

All the women at the table laughed except Jane. It was the truth; Bailey was chasing after anything that had a pair of pants.

"Let her pack your dad's suitcases. You're coming to the club. I'll make Pike dance with you," Sex Piston promised.

"I could help him in the morning..." Jane thought aloud.

"Good, that's settled." Sex Piston beamed at her.

Jane stood up.

"Where you going?"

"I'm going to get me a basket of chicken. I'm hungry."

* * *

Jane wore her black leather leggings and styled her hair that Sex Piston had returned to her normal color of blonde after the trip to Mexico. Then she did her make-up and put on a top that Sex Piston had talked her into buying months ago. It was sexier than anything she usually wore, but she wanted to feel sexy and desirable tonight.

She had come to a decision. Tonight, she was going to get laid. She was going to drive Cade out of her mind by doing another man. The problem was in deciding which one of the brothers she was going to fuck and give her virginity to. She planned on finding one so drunk out of his mind that he wouldn't notice the little detail that it was her first time.

Can guys tell? Jane wondered.

She had never meant to stay a virgin as long as she had. The sad truth was, no man had really put any pressure on her to give it up. They used her to get to the other bitches or her sister. The worst of them, however, were the ones who would act interested only to use her to borrow money.

She had thought a few months ago that she was finally going to lose her ancient cherry. She spent the whole day waxing, doing her hair, painting her nails, all in the effort to spark the guy's desire. Instead, he showed up late, saying he had gotten a flat tire and needed to borrow money for another one. He took the money without even noticing she was wearing a dress and heels, leaving with a brief thanks. The next night, she was leaving the club when she heard him talking to two other brothers, who asked where he got the money for the tire. He told them he got the money from her and then laughed about how she had dressed and lit candles, waiting for him. She still remembered his words.

"Hell, I wouldn't do her for all the money in the world."

"I would," another chimed in, "if I could put a bag over her head."

The men all laughed.

Jane still remembered cringing at their words.

Giving her hair a final pat, she left her bedroom.

"About time," Crazy Bitch said, dusting graham cracker crumbs off her lap. Grabbing one of the lint brushes sitting around the room, she rolled it over her slacks.

"Ready?" Jane asked, going to the door. Killyama was honking the car horn impatiently.

Crazy Bitch threw her a dirty look, slamming the lint brush down, and then they made their way out to Killyama.

They didn't live far from the Destructors' clubhouse. Where the weekend nights were usually packed with the brothers, there seemed to be even more motorcycles than usual tonight.

"Why are there so many here tonight?" Jane asked as she got out of the car.

Crazy Bitch shrugged. "Don't know."

Inside, the clubhouse was filled to capacity, the noise loud and the music blaring.

Killyama waved her hand toward the bar where all their friends were standing in a group with a drink in their hands. T.A. already seemed to be halfway drunk with Bear holding her steady.

"What's going on?" Killyama asked Sex Piston after they had threatened the busy bargirl for a drink.

"The Blue Horsemen are here tonight with some new recruits wanting in. They're going to give them a few tests tonight, so everyone wants to watch."

That explained it. All the brothers liked to challenge the new recruits and to watch them get their asses whipped. The ones who fought the best got the better jobs.

"Where are they?" Crazy Bitch asked as she and Jane both searched the room for new faces.

"They're over at the big table." Sex Piston nodded her head at the table against the wall.

All the women turned to look at the new recruits, and Jane's eyes widened when they were caught and held by a man she had thought she would never see again.

Chapter Sixteen

Cade nodded his head in acknowledgement.

"Fuck," Killyama muttered.

"What's wrong?" Sex Piston looked back and forth between Killyama and Jane.

"That's Cade, the one who saved me and Bailey."

"Which one?" Sex Piston asked, her eyes narrowing on the table.

"The one with dark brown hair and dark eyes." Jane looked away from the table, taking a sip of her beer.

Sex Piston slammed her drink down on the bar and started toward the table, but Jane pulled her back.

"What are you going to do?"

"I'm going to thank him for saving you, and then I'm going to get Stud to kick his ass out of here."

"Don't, Sex Piston," Jane pleaded. "He didn't do anything wrong. I'm the one who wanted him. I should

107

have realized I wasn't his type."

"What the fuck do you mean by that?" Crazy Bitch asked.

Jane gave a self-deprecating smile. "It means I know."

"Know what?" Sex Piston asked.

All her friends looked confused.

"It means I know I'm the ugly one."

"What!"

Jane laid her hand on Sex Piston's arm. "It's the truth, and you all know it. I'm the ugly one in the group. You know, the one who never gets asked to dance or for my number. Men only talk to me to get closer to one of you."

"That's not true," Crazy Bitch chided.

"Yes, it is, and you all know it. It's okay. I'm used to it. Someday, I'll find a guy who thinks I'm the pretty one," she said optimistically, "and won't need to put a bag over my head."

"Fat Louise, that couldn't be further from the truth," Killyama spoke out.

"It's true. I heard Dozer tell Bear that one time."

As the women all stared at Bear accusingly, he turned ashen.

"I think Stud needs something," he mumbled, moving away.

"I'll kill that motherfucker. When I get done with him, he's the one who's going to need a bag." This time, Sex Piston moved toward Dozer, who was unaware of his immediate demise.

"Leave him alone, Sex Piston." Jane clutched her friend's arm tighter. "He just said what everyone else thinks."

"No, they fucking don't," Sex Piston snapped.

"Yes, they do," she said, resigned. "Anyway, I came here to have fun."

The women all grew quiet as Jane climbed onto an empty barstool.

"Are we going to party or not?"

"Hell yes!"

The women climbed up on the stools next to her, and Jane gradually relaxed, loosening up.

After a while, Pike came up behind her. "Want to dance, Fat Louise?"

She slid off the stool. "I would love to."

Jane tried not to feel self-conscious when she saw Cade watching her as they stepped onto the crowded dance floor. Pike talked as they danced, showering her with attention that would normally turn her head. She knew Sex Piston had probably pestered Stud into asking the man to dance with her, but Jane wasn't going to look a gift horse in the mouth. She wanted Cade to think other men found her attractive, even if it wasn't true.

They danced several more songs before they noticed the bikers going outside.

"The fights have started! Let's go watch." Pike grinned.

Jane followed him outside, finding her friends in a place up front.

Recruits were pitted against each other in groups of two. The winners would face off against each other until only four were left. Those four would then take on a member. Those who won their fights would become recruits; those who failed went home with bruises and their tails tucked between their legs.

They weren't invested in the outcome for any of the men, so the women watched silently.

Cade was matched with a man who was twice his size. The recruit was arrogantly confident of himself and swung his fist out, aiming for Cade's jaw. He was stopped mid-swing when Cade grabbed his hand and twisted it behind his back. Cade then threw him away from him, adding to the insult by bringing his boot up to kick him in the ass.

"Show off," Sex Piston grumbled.

The next time Cade was up, he fought someone who was his size. He had removed his shirt, and his upper body had Jane practically drooling, wanting to run her tongue over that six pack he was carrying. Reason returned when she remembered Bailey's gloating look as she had come out of his room.

With his second fight won, he made the final four. He had done it without even breaking a sweat, leaving the other recruit kneeling on the ground, gasping for breath after Cade had fought dirty, punching him in the throat.

Bear took off his own T-shirt before moving to stand in front of Cade. "Try that move with me, fucker, and you're going to be looking in the dirt for your teeth."

Cade laughed at Bear's threat, watching the man intently and waiting for his first move, which was to swing a punch at Cade. When Cade moved, it was into Bear's other fist.

Jane had to look away as Bear landed a few other hard punches before Cade managed to strike him back. When Bear took a step forward to land a hit, Cade's foot swept out, knocking Bear off his feet. Bear started to get up, but Cade circled behind him to place him in a chokehold. It wasn't long before Bear fell forward, unconscious, and then the brothers lifted him out of the way as another fight began.

The other recruits all lost their fights, so Cade was going to be the only new recruit.

The losing men left while the brothers all congratulated Cade, slapping him on his back.

Jane turned away from the sight. She hadn't wanted him to win. Now she was going to have to see him every time she came to the club. How had he even ended up in Jamestown? Had he followed Bailey, not realizing she was only there temporarily?

Jane went back inside with her friends, where they managed to find a table this time.

"I can see why you like him," T.A. enthused. "He's hot."

"I don't like him. I was temporarily in lust with him. I'm over it," Jane lied.

When Sex Piston brought them all drinks, Jane only sipped hers, staring around the club. Pike was hitting the whiskey pretty hard and so was Dozer.

She wasn't going to let Cade change her mind about losing her virginity tonight.

Her decision was made when Pike took the chair next to hers.

"Been drinking a lot tonight," Jane said.

"Celebrating. I landed a new job with more money. I can finally afford that new bike I've been wanting."

Jane saw Cade leaning against the bar, talking to Stud. Turning her chair slightly, she man-aged to put him out of her mind, keeping her attention on Pike.

Sometime later, her full bladder had her excusing herself to go to the restroom. She tried to hurry because the club was filled with horny bitches, and Pike was one of the few men who didn't carry a spare tire around his waist. Most of Stud's men were fit and lean, but the older men, who were original members of the Destructors, had lost their edge long ago.

She left the bathroom, coming to a halt when she saw Cade leaning against the wall.

"Jane."

"Hi, Cade. Everyone calls me Fat Louise here," she told him nervously.

"Never had much ambition to be like everyone else." Cade shrugged.

You've succeeded, Jane thought. He was like no other man she had met before.

"What brought you to Jamestown?"

"Bored with every place else I went and thought I would give this a try."

"If you came to Jamestown to see Bailey again, it's a wasted effort. She and Dad are moving to New York next week."

"Seeing Bailey wasn't an intention of mine."

"Oh." Jane didn't know what else to say. She could

chatter with anyone except Cade; he always made her tongue-tied.

"You with the brother whose dick you were practically ridin' on the dance floor?"

Her mouth dropped open at his remark. "I'm not with anyone," she snapped. "But don't worry, I won't be trying to get your attention like the rest of the bitches out there. I don't share dick with my sister." She threw him a dirty look, turning to leave him in the short hallway. Hopefully, he had received the blunt message that she wasn't mooning over him.

He reached out, grabbing her arm and halting her flight. "What in the fuck are you talking about?"

Chapter Seventeen

"Let go of my arm," Jane snarled.

Close enough to hear Jane's snarl, Sex Piston watched her reaction yet didn't intercede.

Cade released her, and Jane immediately sought to escape. However, he moved to block her, maneuvering her so she was pressed against the wall by his body.

Killyama jumped to her feet, but Sex Piston snagged her hand, jerking her back down.

"Leave them alone."

Killyama looked at Sex Piston in surprise. "I'm going to break his fucking neck," she threatened.

"Let's see what happens. Fat Louise is surrounded by help if she needs it. I'm sick of her moping around after that fucker."

"You want them to get together?" Crazy Bitch asked in dismay.

"I want Jane to get what she wants." Sex Piston stared intently at the couple arguing. It was obvious some shit was going down. If the fucker went too far, she would call a halt and have Stud throw him out of the club. If it didn't, though, Jane might just be able to get the man she couldn't get over.

"If he touches her again, I'm going over there." Killyama folded her arms across her chest, watching them with a narrow-eyed stare.

"Look at her face," Sex Piston said softly.

None of her friends could miss the expression. It was like a kid in a candy store who was afraid to reach out and take the treat she wanted.

"I'll wait." Killyama's begrudging voice brought a sardonic smile to Sex Piston's lips.

"I wouldn't expect any less from you."

* * *

"My dick hasn't been near your sister."

Jane frowned. "Don't lie. I saw her coming out of your hotel room when I came back from looking for the both of you at the restaurant."

Cade scowled. "I never showed up. I went to my room, showered, and passed out on the bed. I was exhausted. I hadn't slept since God knows when, and I didn't wake up until the next morning when I went looking for you. Your dad said you had already left. You didn't even give me a fucking thank you."

"I was going to that night, but I saw Bailey coming from your room. It wasn't exactly the time to burst out my gratitude."

"She was not in my room!"

"Yes, she was! Besides, even if you didn't do her, I saw you putting your hands and mouth on her."

"I did kiss her," Cade admitted. "If she was flirting with me, she wasn't whining over that asshole husband of hers. It was the only way to shut her up until I could get rid of her."

"Oh." Fat Louise bit her lip. "I don't know what to believe."

"Believe me. I'm not attracted to her. You were the one I was attracted to." His knuckles brushed her cheek.

"Why did you come to Jamestown?"

"Found myself bored, and I kept thinking of you. I want to get to know you, Jane."

"Everyone calls me Fat Louise," she reminded him.

His hand curled around the nape of her neck. "You going to let me get to know you better?" he asked, ignoring her reminder.

"I don't know … maybe."

Cade pulled back, laughing. "How about you introduce me to your friends while you're deciding?"

"Okay." Jane smiled up at him.

Leading him back to her table, she introduced him to Sex Piston, Killyama, Crazy Bitch, and T.A. Pike was still sitting there, staring blankly at Cade, drunk off his ass. The thought of him no longer excited Jane; as a result, she revised her plan. Taking a seat at the table, she scooted her chair over so Cade could pull up another one.

"Be right back," she said, going to the bar.

"What's she doing?" asked Crazy Bitch.

"I have no idea." Cade shrugged, surprised when she set a bottle of whiskey down in front of him with a glass.

"Drink up," urged Jane.

Cade stared at Pike then Jane. Opening the bottle, she poured him a generous amount.

"Jane, are you trying to get me drunk?"

"Of course not." Jane felt the tide of red flood her cheeks when she lied.

Cade stared at her skeptically yet reached for his drink.

Crazy Bitch leaned over Cade as if he wasn't there. "You done with Pike?"

Jane nodded.

"Do you mind if I give him a whirl?"

"Help yourself." Jane blushed again at Cade's censoring

115

look.

"Do you and your friends switch men often? I might have a problem with that."

"Don't worry. We'll wait until she's finished with you first." Killyama gave him her killer smile.

"It might be a while." Cade smiled back.

"I'm patient," Killyama quipped.

Jane couldn't believe Killyama was showing Cade her humorous side that she usually only exhibited to her friends.

The atmosphere at the table relaxed as they sat talking about their experience in Mexico. Jane kept Cade's glass filled until he placed his hand over the top, preventing her from pouring more.

"I don't get drunk, Jane."

"You call her Jane?" Sex Piston asked with a raised brow.

"I don't like Fat Louise," Cade answered. "Are you the ones who gave her that nickname?"

"Nope, she did." Sex Piston nodded toward Jane.

She looked down at the table, not meeting Cade's eyes.

"Why?"

At Cade's question, she forced herself to look at him. "Because it reminds me to be strong," Jane said truthfully. Every time she heard that name, it reminded her of all the times she was picked on. To her the nickname was almost a badge of honor. Not to mention God knew she had a hard time refusing food.

She decided to change the subject. "So, you can't get drunk, or you don't let yourself get drunk?"

Cade was silent for a second then sighed. "Never could. I can drink anyone under the table." It wasn't bragging; it was a matter-of-fact statement.

"Okay." Jane stood to her feet, about to leave the table.

"Where are you going now?" Cade stopped her.

"Dozer has some reefer, and Bear has some blow."

Cade's mouth dropped open at her determined attempt

to drug him.

"What's going on, Jane?"

The women at the table cracked up, laughing at him.

"What she's trying not so subtly to do is to take advantage of you," Killyama said, practically falling out of her chair from laughing.

"What?" Cade's astonishment was cut short by Pike breaking into the conservation.

"I'm drunk," he said, nodding his head as he tried to scoot his chair closer to Jane.

Cade jerked Jane onto his lap while using his foot to knock Pike's chair back. Crazy Bitch got up, helping Pike to his feet and then leading the biker away from the table.

Stud came up to the table, standing behind his wife. "Problems?"

"No problems," Sex Piston assured her husband. "You ready to go home?"

"Yeah." Stud looked at Cade. "Where are you staying in town?"

"At the hotel."

"There're a couple of bedrooms empty. Since Ace is not a member anymore, you can have his room. It's the second door on the right."

"Thanks."

"He's going to need it tonight," Sex Piston laughed, getting to her feet.

"Yeah?" Stud gave Cade a hard look.

"No, he's not," Jane denied.

"Don't worry about it. Let's go." Sex Piston took Stud's hand, leading him away.

Jane stayed on Cade's lap, refusing to look at him, with a heated blush on her checks.

Killyama and T.A. both stood up.

"We're going to go dance," Killyama informed them.

"Want to explain?" Cade asked when they were alone.

"No. What I want to do is to get Crazy Bitch and go home."

"Why? Do you only want to have sex with men who are incapacitated? That can't be much fun." The laughter in his voice had her anger rising.

"At least a drunk man wouldn't want me to put a bag over my head. And at least I can get the hell out of there before he wakes up and realizes who he's fucked."

Cade didn't reply. Instead, he stood and carried her to the back of the clubhouse, finding the room Stud had told him he could use. Jane struggled wildly against him. He barely managed to hold on to her long enough to slam the door to the empty bedroom where he dropped her on the bed then took off his shirt and threw it across the room.

"What are you doing?" she shrieked.

"Proving what you just said is bullshit," Cade said grimly, toeing off his boots then pulling off his pants.

Jane lay on the bed, gaping up at him. This was not how she had anticipated her plans going tonight. Not only was it a different man, but he was stone cold sober and furious at her.

"I don't want to fuck now. I'm not in the mood anymore."

"Then I guess it's up to me to put you in the mood."

Chapter Eighteen

Jane stared up at Cade, whose body didn't have an ounce of fat anywhere. His perfection made her even more hesitant.

"Cade, I don't want a mercy fuck."

He dropped down on the bed next to her. "Are you not looking at my dick?" His hand reached out, taking hers and placing it on his hard cock. "Darlin', a man's dick doesn't get this way unless he wants what he's looking at."

Jane let her hand close over the rigid length of his cock, her thumb brushing over the tip, smearing the drop of pre-come.

Cade hissed between gritted teeth, lowering his mouth to cover hers. He thrust his tongue inside, ravaging her mouth in a passionate kiss that had her head falling back to the mattress.

Slowly, her hand slid along his cock, investigating the

size and texture of something she had been dreaming about since she had met him.

Cade groaned out, "If you don't stop, I'm going to come." He pried her hand away before raising it above her head, keeping it pinned in place. Then one of Cade's thighs parted her legs.

Her shirt had come up when she landed on the bed, and his hand now flattened across her stomach before sliding under her leggings. Cade moved his fingers toward her pussy as Jane arched her hips, even before he touched her. When he finally did, she groaned at the intimate touch as he circled her clit before rubbing it with his calloused fingers, stimulating her into wrapping her leg around him, opening herself to his explorations.

"You lied," Cade mocked, breaking the kiss.

"About what?"

"Being in the mood. You're so wet I could slide my dick right in without the foreplay."

"I like the foreplay." Jane tried to catch his mouth again, but Cade had moved on, letting her hand go to raise her top.

"Jesus." Cade's mouth went to the already tight tip, sucking her nipple into his mouth while his fingers moved faster against her.

Jane moaned at the added stimulation, moving against him as her stomach clenched and the sensations in her pussy grew more frantic.

Cade then pulled his hand away, sitting up.

"You're stopping?" Jane was brought out of her lust-induced haze to see Cade sliding off the bed.

"Are you out of your fucking mind? No, I'm not stopping. I'm going to take off those pants so I can fuck you." Cade's hands went to her boots, jerking them off, before sliding her leggings off her hips and throwing them on the floor. Then he lifted her slightly and practically ripped her out of her shirt.

"Thank God you didn't get me drunk."

"Why?"

"Because I wouldn't have remembered the way you look. You're the sexiest thing I've ever seen." He placed a knee on the bed, about to climb back on when Jane placed her hand on his chest.

"You don't have to lie." Jane licked her full bottom lip. "I know I'm not pretty or sexy like the other women."

"No, you're not."

Jane felt a flash of hurt at his quick agreement.

"You're prettier and sexier than them." He took her hands back in his, pinning them above her head as he settled between her thighs. "Your tits are firm with cherry red nipples, just the way I like." His tongue circled each nipple, giving them attention. "Your skin is soft, and your body is strong, with enough flesh to grip while I fuck you." Cade kept her hands pinned above her head with one hand, the other one putting his cock at her entrance.

"Aren't you going to wear a condom?" Jane panted.

"I'm clean. I haven't fucked anyone without a condom since I was sixteen. You on the pill?"

"Yes." Jane had gone on it months ago when she had decided she wasn't going to be a virgin by her birthday. Her birthday had come and gone, while her virginity had remained intact.

"Then, no, I'm not going to wear a condom." Cade's voice tautened as he slid his cock inside her silky pussy, bracing his weight on one hand.

He tried to enter her slick warmth in one stroke yet was stopped. He looked at Jane who was biting her bottom lip, trying not to grimace. She had pasted a smile on her face when he stopped to stare down at her.

"Don't stop. It feels so good."

"Don't you dare tell me something feels good when I'm having sex with you and it doesn't. I know I'm hurting you."

Cade bent down and gently licked her bottom lip. "Do you know why men stare at you?"

Jane nodded, feeling her insecurities rise.

Cade laughed, shaking his head. "Darlin', all a man can think about when he looks at you is that mouth sucking his dick. Hell, I want to come just thinking about your mouth sucking me while I play with your pussy or tits."

Jane felt a rush of warmth between her thighs at his dirty talk as he went on to describe how she would give him a blowjob. As he talked, his mouth lowered to her nipple, playing with the tight tip as his hips pushed his cock higher inside her. She gave a slight wince when he finally thrust all the way inside her pussy.

Cade sucked her nipple into his mouth again, biting down on the tip as his hips began moving back and forth. The erotic feel of being open to him was like nothing Jane had imagined, nor were the feelings of frenzied need.

He was going too slowly to satisfy the desires that were building like an unquenchable fire. When Jane tore her hands free, grabbing his ass to pull him tighter against her, Cade took the hint, moving more forcefully. Jane arched under his body as she finally felt her orgasm tear through her body while Cade's cock jerked within her, releasing his own.

"You going to let me go?" Cade's amused voice had her releasing her tight grip on his ass.

He moved to the side, lifting both of them to lie against the pillows at the head of the bed.

"I need to go find Crazy Bitch. She's probably wondering where I am," Jane said, snuggling against his side.

"She saw me bring you back here."

"She did?"

Cade nodded his head. "I'll take you home in the morning."

"You want me to stay?"

"I'm not done with you tonight." Cade smiled down at her as he reached out to play with one of her nipples.

"Are you sure?" Jane asked.

"I'm sure. I have several positions I want to initiate you into, and then I'm going to show you how to give me a blowjob."

"I'm a fast learner," Jane quipped, thankful he wasn't making a big deal about taking her virginity.

"Darlin', there's not going to be anything fast about what we're going to be doing."

Chapter Nineteen

Jane had Crazy Bitch call Killyama to drop her off at her father's house after Cade had taken her home that morning. She let herself into her father's house. She had called him last night to tell him she would come by this morning, but he hadn't answered his phone. She had checked her phone this morning for any messages from him, yet he hadn't replied. Worried, she had stupidly forgotten her phone in Cade's bedroom. Now he had no way to reach her.

Her good mood disappeared when she walked inside her father's house and saw him sitting white-faced on a chair in his living room while Bailey sat on the couch crying.

"What's wrong? Did something happen?" Concerned, she stared back and forth between her father and sister.

"We're broke!" Bailey wailed.

Jane took a seat on the couch, although she didn't try to comfort her sister.

"What happened?" Jane asked, startled by the change in her father's finances.

"Bailey didn't take Raul's name off her accounts and emails. Raul has managed to steal almost every dime of my money. He gained access through her accounts."

"Don't blame me. I forgot. You should have reminded me." Bailey, as always, deflected the blame to someone else.

"I didn't realize anything was wrong until I bought our new house and the sale couldn't go through, because there was a lack of funds," their father continued, ignoring Bailey.

"I'm sorry." Jane didn't know what else to say. "What are you going to do?"

"The banks are trying to find a way to get my money back, but with Raul and the money both in Mexico, it's going to be impossible. I'll have to go back to work fulltime, obviously, and Bailey will have to find a job. I won't be able to give you an allowance any longer, either."

"That's all right. I just gave it to Bailey and Mom, anyway. I've been supporting myself for years."

"Why would you give it to Bailey? She had her own allowance, and your mother is more than able to get a job."

"Bailey always spent her allowance before the middle of the month, and Mom doesn't want to work. I guess now she'll have to." Jane dreaded telling her mother that piece of news.

"I can't get a job. What would I do?" Bailey looked at her father frantically.

"Yes, you can, and you will. You have no choice; neither do I. I'll be starting over from scratch, and I'm not young anymore. Thank God this house is paid for, or we would be homeless."

"You wouldn't be homeless. You could have stayed

with me and Crazy Bitch."

From his expression, Jane was sure he would rather be homeless.

"I'm not qualified for anything," Bailey protested.

"Popeye's is hiring, and they'll train you," Jane suggested.

Bailey stared at her angrily. "I wouldn't work at a fast food restaurant."

"Good luck finding something in Jamestown, then. It took me over a year to get hired at the hospital."

"I'll call some friends of mine. Maybe they'll have some suggestions." Bailey flounced out of the room, leaving Jane and her father alone.

"Is there anything I can do?" she offered.

"No, but thanks for offering instead of yelling at me." Jane could only imagine her sister's reaction when she had been told. "The only bright spot is that your stepmother's not going to get the large settlement she thought she was out of our divorce."

Jane felt bad for her father. Not knowing what else to do, she fixed them both lunch and sat talking with him until he told her he needed to make his own phone calls to work on getting his fulltime job back.

She went upstairs in search of her sister, finding her in her bedroom, sprawled on a chaise lounge. She was talking on her cell phone, which she hung up when she saw Jane enter the room.

"Next time, knock," Bailey snapped.

Surprisingly, she didn't look upset any longer; instead, she appeared to have been put in a better frame of mind by whomever she had been on the phone with.

"I want to talk to you." Jane hesitated, but she wanted answers badly enough to put up with her sister's caustic attitude.

"So talk."

"Why did you act like you had slept with Cade that night at the hotel?"

Bailey gave an unconcerned shrug at being caught in the lie. "Because I knew you wanted him," she said truthfully. "I knew you were about to make a fool of yourself over him, so I stopped you."

"So you did it to save me from myself?" Jane said doubtfully.

"Of course. What other reason could there be?" Bailey stood, hugging Jane. "You're my sister; it's my job to watch out for you."

"It wasn't because you wanted him?" Jane had been around her sister too long to believe in her sincerity.

"Maybe I was a little attracted. He took my mind off Raul, but then he disappeared the next day, so it really doesn't matter anymore, does it?"

"I guess not." Jane couldn't explain why she didn't want Bailey to know Cade was in Jamestown, only that she didn't.

"Good. No hard feelings?"

"Of course not," Jane lied. She had learned a lesson about her sister: there was no length to the deception she would go to in order to get what she wanted. It was a lesson that couldn't be unlearned.

She said goodbye to Bailey and headed back downstairs to see her father had finished making his calls.

Jane kissed him on his cheek as she was about to leave.

"Call me if you need me for anything." She went to the door, hearing Killyama blowing her horn.

"Jane…" He seemed about to say something, but then only said, "I'll see you soon."

She left, feeling bad for her dad and wishing there was something she could do. Then an idea came to her on the ride home.

"Could you take me somewhere else first?"

* * *

Cade leaned against the bar, looking around the room. He saw Crazy Bitch and T.A., but he didn't see Jane. He had tried calling her several times during the day, but she hadn't answered.

Stud took a seat on the stool next to him. "Who are you looking for?"

"Jane. I thought she was coming in with Crazy Bitch tonight," Cade told him, still watching the door.

"Not tonight. She's in Treepoint with Killyama and Sex Piston. They're having dinner with a friend of theirs."

"Oh." Jane hadn't mentioned that when he had taken her home this morning.

"She might stop by when they come back." Stud shot him a calculating look. "You know Sex Piston and Fat Louise are close."

"That would be hard to miss," Cade remarked.

Stud gave him a warning look. "Fat Louise isn't like the rest of the bitches. Her friends usually close ranks around her to keep her safe. I would really hate it if Sex Piston starts busting my balls about how you're treating her."

"Are you warning me to stay away from her?" Cade stiffened, preparing himself for an argument. He liked Stud, respected him as a leader of his men, but he wasn't going to quit seeing Jane on his say so.

"Fuck no. What I'm saying is to play fair with her. If you just want her as a fuck toy, she needs to know that up front. If you plan on her becoming your old lady, then be honest about that, too. What I don't want is to hear my wife bitching at me that you broke Fat Louise's heart. I wouldn't be happy about that. I kinda like her. She's good to my kids."

Cade felt a smile tugging at his lips. "I'll keep that in mind. To be honest, I don't know where this is going with Jane. When she left after we were rescued, I missed her. I got used to having her around, didn't have any desire to fuck my usual women. After a while of that shit, a man can get worried."

"Last night take that worry off your mind?"

"Yes, it did," Cade laughed.

"It was the same before I started seeing Sex Piston.

Club pussy just didn't do it for me anymore."

"That's hard to imagine." Cade looked at the provocatively dressed women sitting around the club.

"Like I said, make sure Jane doesn't get hurt. There are a few brothers who feel the same." With that, Stud took his beer, leaving him standing alone at the bar.

Talking with Stud had made Cade even more pissed that Jane was ignoring his calls while he was sitting around like a pussy waiting for her to come around. Fuck that!

He began talking to a seductive blond who sidled up close to him. She was curvy, and her tits under her low cut T-shirt drew his eyes several times. When he reached for his drink, his elbow brushed against her breasts. Waiting for a signal from his dick that he was ready to party, he was disappointed when he didn't feel a stir like he had just by looking at Jane.

Just then, his eyes were caught and held by Crazy Bitch. He could tell he had gone down in her estimation. Well, if she already thought less of him, better make it worthwhile.

Turning his back to the room, he wrapped his arms around the blond, pulling her close for a kiss, hoping his dick would stand up and take notice.

Cade had thought when he fucked Jane he would get her out of his system; instead, he was even worse off than before. He had always been able to fuck women out of his mind. He couldn't remember ever being with a woman more than a couple of times. As soon as he discovered what they were like in bed, his interest would wane. Then he would be on top of another woman, discovering the delights of a new pussy. Maybe he just needed to fuck her a couple more times, and then the attraction she held for him would disappear.

Sometime later, the blonde's eyes widened as she stared over his shoulder. Cade casually turned his head, coming face-to-face with an angry Sex Piston while Jane stood behind her, trying to tug her away.

"You never learn, do you, Demie?" Sex Piston snarled

at the woman who was turning a sickly shade of green.

There was no way to miss the hurt look in Jane's eyes. He felt a small clench in his chest.

"I haven't touched Stud, and Cade doesn't belong to you."

"No, he doesn't, but he does to Fat Louise."

"No, he doesn't. Let's go, Sex Piston." Jane tried to pull her friend away.

Sex Piston jerked her arm away from Jane, and then Cade heard Demie's running footsteps behind his back.

"Didn't take you long to start sniffing after the club whores," Sex Piston snapped.

"Maybe, if Fat Louise answered her phone, I wouldn't have."

While Jane flinched when he called her by her nickname, Cade thought for a second that Sex Piston was going to hit him. Surprisingly, Jane moved to stand in front of Sex Piston, blocking her.

"Stop it," she told her furious friend before turning to Cade. "I left my phone in your room this morning. When you find it, give it to Stud for me."

"Jane…" Cade's anger evaporated, and he reached out to touch her.

"Let me save you the trouble, Cade. We fucked, and now you want something new. No hard feelings." She turned to a seething Sex Piston. "I'm ready to go home."

Cade watched the group of women leave the club. Demie came sidling back as soon as they left. As her hands curled around his waist, Cade tried to convince himself it was better he hadn't become more involved with Jane. After a good night's sleep, he would take off on his bike and leave Jamestown and Jane behind him.

Chapter Twenty

Cade walked into the clubroom to make himself a cup of coffee. Usually deserted at this time of morning, the room was filled with the brothers eating from take-out bags Stud was placing on the bar counter.

Cade nabbed himself a cup of coffee as he took a seat on one of the stools next to Stud. "What has everyone up so early?" he asked, taking the lid off the coffee that had nearly burned the skin off his tongue.

"My brother Calder gets out of prison today," Stud answered, reaching for his own coffee then taking a seat next to him. "It's been awhile since we've seen him. He did three months in rehab then had to do some time in prison for breaking his parole. The brothers and I are going to be his welcoming committee."

"That and make sure he doesn't get himself back in prison before the day's out," Rock said as he took one of the take-out bags and then left the two men alone after the hard stare Stud gave him.

"You look like shit."

Cade shrugged. "Late night."

"I saw the empty bottle of Tequila when you went to your room with Gina. Between you and the bitches, I can't keep enough Tequila in stock." Stud studied him out of the corner of his eye.

Cade changed the subject, not wanting to give him any information he could give his wife. He had never been one to confide and didn't see the need to now, especially when he would come out looking like a dumbass to the woman he wasn't getting over as easily as he had thought he would.

"Mind if I tag along?"

Stud stood up, slapping him on his back so hard he nearly knocked him off the stool.

"Not at all. I was going to ask if you wanted to ride. Let's hit the road!"

The men left the bar with Cade hoping his piece of shit bike made it. He was going to have to do something about it soon because it was becoming more trouble to hang on to than his bike was worth. It had too many miles and repairs needed to make it through another ride across the country.

Cade climbed onto the old Victory and started the reluctant motor.

"Try to keep up," Rock jibed as they rode out.

Cade's hands tightened on his handlebars, wanting to reach his booted foot out to kick Rock's bike. However, he knew the insult would start a fight, and he didn't want to hold Stud up from being there when his brother was released.

It took over an hour for them to ride to the prison where the bikers parked by the gate.

Cade had done a year himself when he was younger and knew the feelings the man exiting was experiencing.

The two brothers resembled each other in their facial features, but that was where the similarities ended. The hardened features and glacial eyes didn't mirror Stud's more laid back attitude, and Calder's hair was lighter. Stud always kept his face shaved, while Calder had a beard. Stud was taller, but Calder was heavier. He had used his time inside to work out. Cade knew it was to pass the time and keep himself from being a bitch to the other prisoners. It was a dog eat dog world inside prison—a place where the strong survived, and the weak were fucked.

Cade stood as the brothers greeted their friend.

Stud stepped away from his brother after giving him a bear hug that lifted him off his feet.

"Motherfucker, it's good to see you again," Calder spoke as he looked at the brothers surrounding him.

"Glad you're finally out, brother. Let's go home. Dozer rode your bike down for you." Stud tossed him the keys as they walked back to the bikes.

"Does that mean I have to ride with the fucker at my back to the clubhouse?"

Cade looked at the pained expression on Dozer's face.

"Hell no. Had the bitches drop off a car for him to drive back to town." Stud laughed.

Calder sat on his bike then caught Cade staring at him.

"I see we have some new brothers." Calder nodded his head at Cade while he talked to Stud as if Cade wasn't sitting only a few inches away.

"That's Cade. He's not brother yet, but he saved one of the bitches. Trying to make him feel at home while he decides if he wants to join or not."

"He ride with you today?"

"Yeah," Stud answered.

"He fucking the bitches, drinking our liquor?"

"Yeah," Stud repeated the same answer.

"He defend the club's honor?"

"He kicked a local's ass for calling Bear a fart blossom, so yeah, he's defended the club's honor."

"Sound's like he's made his mind up already." Calder started his bike. "I need a fucking beer and to get laid."

"I'll get you the beer; you'll have to find the other one yourself," Stud joked.

"Gina still hanging around the club?"

"Yeah, brother, she's still there."

"Problem solved."

"She might be a little tired. I left her sleeping in my bed," Cade told him, wondering if he had fucked the man's woman.

Calder gave him a shit-eating grin. "Then I'll wake her up with a present. Santa's coming early for her."

"You sure one bitch is going to be enough?" Stud quipped.

"For now. I want to see my nieces and nephew before I get started with the whores and liquor."

Cade caught an inexplicable expression cross Stud's face at Calder's words.

"We'll stop by Sex Piston's parents' house first. She's there with the kids."

"Shit, Sizzle know I'm coming?"

"I told her yesterday."

"Fuck, she probably made me a cake."

Cade couldn't understand why the man looked so upset about someone making a cake for him, but he didn't have time to question any of the brothers as they drove away from the prison.

He thought the brothers would pull away and head back to the clubhouse when Calder and Stud turned down a side street. When they pulled in front of a house, he remained sitting with the other brothers while Stud and Calder went inside.

Cade's head turned when he saw movement on the side of the house. Jane was playing with a little girl who was running around the yard. She ran up behind the squealing little girl who laughed when Jane tossed her into the air then deftly caught her. Placing the small girl on her hip, she sat down on a swing with the child on her lap. Jane was talking softly to the little girl while running her hands through her hair. When the little girl tried to wiggle free, Jane reached into her pocket and pulled out a candy bar. Breaking it in two pieces, she gave one to the child. They sat quietly, eating their treat.

"Don't go there, brother." Cade turned his head at Bear's comment.

"What the fuck does that mean?"

"It means you were smart enough to walk away once. Dozer almost fell for her, but he put the emergency brake on."

"Dozer and Jane were together?" Cade asked sharply.

"No, he wanted a fuck; she wanted something more. Dozer didn't want any woman to have him by the balls, though. She's the type that gets under your skin and doesn't let go. Hell, there's not a brother here who hasn't imagined their dick in her mouth, until she talks and ruins it. When I want a piece of tail, I don't want to fuck Marsha Brady."

Cade barely held his fury in check at the way Bear was talking about Jane.

"A man would have to hide her face to be able to walk away from that sweet piece. The brothers and I all like variety. Besides, Sex Piston would castrate any brother who did her girl wrong." Bear stared at Jane with a wistful expression. "There's two types of women men like us need to stay away from."

"What are they?" Cade asked, becoming amused by Bear's forlorn expression.

"One is a woman who makes you think of home and kids. The second is the kind who twists your nuts into a knot."

"Which type is Jane?"

"Brother, she's both."

* * *

"Can I have a Miller Lite?" Cade heard Jane ask Stud,

who was standing behind the bar for the beer.

"Sorry, Fat Louise, I just gave Bear the last one."

Cade was standing at the bar with Calder, Dozer, Bear, and Gina. Demie was sitting on a stool next to them. When Stud told her he didn't have the beer, she gave a pretty pout that had Cade's cock twitching in his jeans.

She was dressed in a cream sweater that was loose and fell off her smooth shoulder and dark leggings that were covered by a tiny black skirt. She looked sexy as fuck.

Bear, who had been about to raise his beer to his mouth, paused before handing it to her. Jane's silvery eyes glowed with happiness, as if he had given her a damn diamond ring.

"Thanks, Bear," she said, taking the beer. "Crazy Bitch will appreciate it."

Cade almost laughed out loud at Bear's expression.

"You have food at the table?" Stud questioned sharply.

Cade thought Stud was overly concerned about Jane drinking on an empty stomach.

"Yes, Crazy Bitch brought us all sandwiches from the Vegan Factory."

"Cool."

"Can I get a bottled water?"

"Sure thing." Stud handed her one.

As she turned away from the bar, their eyes met before she jerked her gaze away, catching Calder's.

"Hey, Calder, it's nice seeing you again." Her honeyed voice had his balls clenching into a vice.

"Hi, Fat Louise. You're looking sexy as usual. Makes me realize what I was missing in prison." Calder took a step forward, grabbing her to pull her into his body, hugging her close as his hands went to her ass.

Cade couldn't prevent his jaw clenching when he saw the blatant sexual touch.

Jane merely laughed, pushing him away and then nodding her head towards Gina and Demie. "I see you're making up for lost time."

"You know it." Calder's expression darkened as he lifted the bottle of whiskey he was holding to his mouth.

Cade couldn't hide his countenance quick enough to prevent Calder from seeing his reaction.

"Well, enjoy yourself." Jane left the men all staring as she walked away, clutching the drinks in a tight grip.

Calder placed his arm around Gina's shoulder yet looked towards Cade.

"We gonna have a problem if I take Gina out back?"

"Hell no. You can fuck your brains out with any bitch here, and I wouldn't care," Cade answered him. The exception being the woman he was still watching walk away, Cade thought to himself.

Calder stared back at him astutely. "Is that so?"

"Yeah."

"In that case"—he placed his other arm around Demie as she slid from the stool—"like Fat Louise said, I'm going to make up for lost time. But I'm not a brother who minds sharing."

"Me, either." Cade placed his beer on the counter before following Calder from the clubroom, unable to keep his gaze from Jane's table as he passed.

She refused to glance up, but her friends at the table gave him disgusted looks. Although they couldn't be more disgusted with him than he was with himself. Still, he didn't stop going in the direction he was heading, despite knowing nothing was going to happen in the bedroom that could compare to the night he had shared with Jane.

When he had been a kid growing up in Arizona, his mother had made him stand next to her as she stood on a corner holding a sign "My son is hungry." He had been forced to stand there without shoes on because she said it made people feel sorry for them. In the burning heat, she had begged for money to feed her and his father's habit. Even now, he remembered the burning heat scorching his bare feet until he couldn't take it any longer, and his mother would let him stand in the shade until the stoplight turned red. The humiliation burned almost as badly as the pavement as they handled those who gave them money, forced to endure their pitying gazes until he had grown too large to generate their sympathy.

Life hadn't become any easier after that. He had taken a job in a local restaurant as a dish-washer until he had graduated high school. He had sworn as he had stood at that metal sink that, when he turned eighteen, he would leave and never look back at the family he left behind, never let himself be tied down with feeling responsible for anyone again. He had lived by that code ever since, and he had never regretted it once.

Until now.

Chapter Twenty-one

Cade pulled his bike into the small gas station. Looking around, he saw the gas pumps didn't take credit cards and the station itself was run down.

Getting off his bike, he walked toward the open bay, seeing Stud working on a bike.

"Hey, Stud."

Stud paused with the wrench in his hand. "What brings you out here?"

Cade moved closer to the bike Stud was working on. "My bike is a piece of shit. Dozer told me you built the one you ride. That's a nice one you're working on now."

Stud stood up, picking up a shop rag to wipe his hands. "It's already sold. I make custom bikes, but I only build two a year. This year's orders have already been taken and paid for."

Cade stared down at the beautiful bike. It might be

worth waiting around for, although he had already stayed in town four months longer than he had thought he would. Each day, he had woken with the intent of getting on his bike and leaving; instead, he had found some lame excuse to stay for another day.

He had never stayed in one place as long as he had Jamestown. He felt the burning need to put Jamestown behind him, yet he hadn't left, placing most of the blame on a bike that had more mechanical problems than it was worth. If he was going to hit the road, he needed a new bike.

"I couldn't talk you into doing three?"

"My bikes are expensive," Stud warned.

Cade's lips twitched. "I think I can afford it."

Stud went to an old refrigerator and pulled out two beers, tossing one to Cade. "Christmas is coming up in a few months, and I have four kids and Sex Piston to buy for. I can build you one next. Rock isn't expecting his until March."

Cade stiffened when he heard Rock's name. The Blue Horseman was from the West Virginia chapter, but since Pike had transferred for a new job, Rock had moved to the Jamestown chapter to replace Pike. He was a nice guy, but the beef he had with Rock was Jane. The brother was on her like flies on shit.

"I'd appreciate it," Cade said, opening his beer and taking a drink while Stud studied him quizzically.

"You got a beef with Rock?"

Cade guessed he hadn't hidden his reaction to Rock's name. "No beef."

"Sure," Stud laughed, setting his beer down on the worktable. "Way you've been hitting the sheets with every bitch in the club, you can't blame Fat Louise for getting her some, too."

"Is she getting any?" Cade asked, despite himself.

Stud paused for a split second as a look Cade couldn't decipher came over his face. "I don't know, brother. You'll have to take that up with her. I learned long ago to keep my nose out of the business of the brothers and the bitches."

Cade nodded his head, setting his own beer down on the worktable. "Let me know how much I owe you for the bike, and I'll get the cash for you."

"Will do. Be careful riding that piece of shit until I can get yours built."

"I will."

"You going to hit the road as soon as it's done?"

"Yeah. Hung around here too long already."

"You don't like Jamestown?" Stud began working on the bike again.

"I like it too much, but I travel, it's what I do. Left home the day I turned eighteen, joined the Marines, did my time in the service, and got out. There are a lot of jobs open for a man who wants to sell his skills to the right buyer. Moved from town to town, taking the jobs I wanted, and I turned down those I didn't. I made enough a couple of years ago to retire, and the job I took for Jane's father was just icing on the cake."

"Ever go back to see your parents?"

"Fuck no. My old man was a junkie who knocked me around whenever he wanted, and my ma stood back and watched. Don't even know if they're alive or dead; don't care enough to find out, either."

"Don't guess I blame you." Stud reached for the wrench. "Ever think the reason you're a nomad is because you're searching for a family that'll have your back?"

"No. Don't want a family. They tie you down and destroy you."

"On the other hand, they can have your back when no one else will. The Blue Horsemen and the Destructors have your back, whether you want them to or not, so you might as well learn to live with that fact, brother."

* * *

Cade went back to the clubhouse with Stud's words

141

repeating over and over in his mind. He had drawn closer to the brothers over the past months, despite himself. He refused to acknowledge Jane had any part in his staying. Even if she did, it wouldn't have mattered. He wasn't ready to stop roaming, and from the expression on her face that day, she had been cut hard by his actions. Wounds like that didn't heal overnight, if ever.

He needed a fucking drink to take her image out of his mind. The other women he had found himself with since then had failed to do so. Cade didn't think the liquor would help any better, although he was at a point where he was willing to try anything to drive the feel of her away for a few minutes.

Going to the bar, he stood next to Dozer and Bear. Both were arguing back and forth on who they were going to fuck that evening.

A little while later, the door opened, and Sex Piston and her crew came in with Stud. Cade admired the man who was able to handle being around the women constantly.

He noticed Jane wasn't with the crew again that night. He hadn't seen her in a couple of months. At first, when he had made an ass of himself, she had come to the club every night with one of the bitches in tow, as if to show him she didn't give a shit, but her visits had gradually tapered off until she never showed at all anymore.

Stud left the women sitting at a table and came to the bar. "June, give me drinks for the girls, and I'll take a whiskey. I need it." Stud winked at the brunette, whose tits were showing through the white T-shirt she was wearing.

The clubhouse door opened, and Jane's father came inside looking like he had the first time Cade had met him, like he was so scared he was about to shit himself.

"What's he doing here?" Cade asked Stud, who gave him another weird look that he couldn't decipher. Cade was beginning to get the feeling that something was going on he didn't know about.

He watched as Montgomery approached Sex Piston's table.

"Sex Piston, I've been looking for Jane. Where is she?"

"Why do you give a shit?"

Montgomery was obviously startled by her harsh question. "She's my daughter, and I haven't seen or heard from her in over two months."

"And you're just now getting worried? Fuck off!" Sex Piston snarled.

"I'll call the police and report her missing!"

"Call them. I'll tell them she's working at Popeye's, on top of her hospital job."

"What? Why is she working there?"

"Because she's trying to keep a roof over her sorry mother's head."

"But I succeeded in getting my money back, and I made sure her allowance was restarted."

"Look in the account, and you'll see she doesn't touch it. She doesn't want a dime of your money, never has. That's why she's always given it to her mom and that bitch daughter of yours."

"Why wouldn't she...? I don't understand."

"Because, what did you do when you got your money back two months ago? You and Bailey went running back to New York. Who the fuck do you think got that money back for you?"

"The banks—"

"Bullshit. Those banks didn't give a fuck whether you recovered your money or not. Jane went to The Last Riders and asked for their help. Knox is a computer engineer, and Crash is a computer nerd. They stole the money back for you."

"I didn't know."

"Jesus! You're so fucking stupid. How did you make that money in the first place?"

"I need to go see her..." Montgomery turned yet was stopped by Sex Piston's harsh words.

"Stay the fuck away from her. She doesn't want to see you right now or anyone else who's hurt her. She wants to be left alone. You go near her, and I'll kick your ass."

"Is she in trouble? I can help—"

"You can't help her now. It's too fucking late." Sex Piston's voice grew tight. Cade had a feeling he wasn't going to like what came out of her mouth next. "You've never been a father to her. You left her behind then flaunted that blond bitch in front of her as the daughter you loved and cared about more. When she was a teenager, you let her stepmother and Bailey both torment her about her looks until she started calling herself the name they would call her when you weren't around. Only when Bailey took off did you remember you have another daughter.

"When Bailey disappeared, you made sure to let Jane know how upset you were that she was in danger, leaving no doubt in Jane's mind that you wished it was her instead of Bailey. She even knows that, when Cade asked you who to save if it came down to the two of them, he was to leave Jane to die and save Bailey!" Sex Piston's voice rose until she was yelling at the ashen man.

"How does she know that?"

"Because you told your wife, and she relayed it to Bailey, who threw it up to Jane, you fucking asshole! If someone asked me that fucking question, I would have shot them then found someone else to do the job. Get out of my face before I beat the shit out of you."

Montgomery grabbed onto the back of a chair. Cade wasn't sure if it was more to hold himself up or to use in self-defense if Sex Piston decided to attack.

"I have to go see her to make things right."

"You're never going to make things right for her. Right now, dealing with you is the last thing she needs or wants. She had a miscarriage and needs peace right now, and I'm going to see she gets it. Go back to New York and wait a few months. Maybe then she'll be more able to deal with your guilty conscience."

"She was pregnant? Who…?"

"It doesn't matter who the father was. He didn't care about her any more than you do. Get out!" Sex Piston lunged to her feet, and both Killyama and Crazy Bitch held her back as Montgomery fled the club. Cade stood as still as if someone had punched him in the gut. "It was mine, wasn't it?" he asked Stud hoarsely.

"Yeah, brother, it was your kid."

Chapter Twenty-two

Jane filled the large cup with soda then snapped on the lid. Looking at her watch, she saw she had thirty minutes left on her shift. She had already finished her clean up, so she would only have to clock out when her shift was over.

Carrying the drink to the counter, she handed it to the man waiting.

"Thanks." Rock took the drink, giving her a smile.

"You're welcome." He always stopped by at the end of each night to give her a ride home. Jane appreciated him offering. She had hated to call Killyama when he was already here, so she had accepted the rides. "I won't be much longer."

"Take your time. I'll sit at a table until you're ready."

"Okay." Jane gave him a smile as he moved away.

"Jane, can you box up the rest of the chicken?" Corra, the manager, asked.

"Sure." Jane turned her back to the counter and started boxing up the fried chicken that hadn't been sold.

Corra let the workers take home what they wanted, and Jane could now say she was sick of her favorite meal. She couldn't choke down another piece of chicken if someone put a gun to her head.

She was almost done when she heard the bell ring over the door.

"Hold off on boxing the chicken. We may need to drop some more." Jane turned around at Corra's order, seeing the mass of large bikers entering the restaurant.

"Call the cops and tell them to do a swing by," Corra muttered under her breath.

"It's okay. I know them." Jane's words didn't take the frown off her manager's face.

Dozer was the first in line to place his order, but Jane's attention was on Cade who stepped to the counter in front of her.

"We need to talk."

"No, we don't." Jane ignored him, going to stand beside Corra.

Looking at the screen, she began filling Dozer's order. She boxed his chicken and sides, placing them on a tray to hand to Corra. She continued to avoid Cade who was standing grimly in place when she went to fix Dozer's soda. Her hand shook as she snapped on the lid. Carrying it carefully, she placed it down on the counter, afraid she would make a fool of herself and drop it. Cade merely stood with his arms crossed over his chest as he waited while she filled the orders.

The small restaurant was practically filled with the bikers. Jane was sure no other customers could come inside with the parking lot filled with motorcycles.

She went back and forth behind the counter, noticing that Corra was becoming more agitated with Cade watching her.

"Will you go away?" Jane hissed at him.

"No."

"Jane," Corra called to her as Jane shot Cade a nasty look. "You can go ahead and leave. Jake and I can finish up."

"But I have fifteen more minutes."

"Don't worry about it. I'll clock you out. Just go."

Jane could tell she was better off not arguing. She went to the back and grabbed her purse before returning to the front. Stepping out from behind the counter, her path was blocked by Cade as he took her arm.

"Let me go," Jane protested.

"We're going to talk."

"Let her go." Rock came to her side.

"Back off, Rock. Jane has something she needs to tell me."

Jane went white at his words. He had found out. One of her big mouthed friends must have told him about the miscarriage.

"I did have something to tell you, but now I don't. I don't know why you're upset, anyway. It's not like it would have mattered to you. You're too busy getting laid and riding that bike around town with the brothers."

Cade flinched at her words.

"It matters. It was my baby, too."

"Not anymore," Jane choked out.

Rock placed his arm around Jane, and she leaned against him for support, suddenly feeling dizzy.

"Take me home, Rock."

"Brother, I'm giving you a warning. Take your arm off her, or we're going to have a problem."

"The only problem I see is a man who wants something back he threw away." Rock didn't take his arm away as he moved Jane so she was on his other side, farther away from Cade.

"I didn't throw shit away. I screwed up."

"What's the fucking difference?"

"This is a talk me and Jane need to be having, not you

and me, Rock."

"Do you want to talk to him?" Rock questioned Jane.

"No." Jane only wanted to get out of there and go to bed. She was exhausted. She needed to get some sleep before she had to be back at work at the hospital at six a.m.

"That settles it. Move, Cade," Rock ordered.

"Make me."

"Cade, stop it. I'm tired—" Jane began.

"Are you always going to hide behind someone, Jane? When are you…?"

Jane felt his words fade out as the room began spinning. The last thing she heard was Cade's shout.

* * *

Jane moved her head on the pillow, staring at the man lying next to her. She was in her bedroom at Crazy Bitch's apartment, having no idea how she had gotten there.

"Good, you're awake." Cade sat up on the bed, staring down at her.

"What happened?"

"You passed out."

"I did?"

"Yes. Thank God Killyama came in when she did. She got the gel out of your purse. Why didn't you tell me you're hypoglycemic? Why didn't I notice in Mexico?"

"Because it's none of your business." Then sighed seeing he expected an explanation. "I carried glucose gel in my pocket."

"Do you know how fucking irresponsible it was not to tell me? Why couldn't you have just told me? Why do you have a problem telling me shit I should know, like being pregnant with my child?"

Jane turned her head on the pillow to avoid looking at his face. "I was going to tell you. I had only found out I was pregnant a few weeks before I lost the baby."

"You should have told me as soon as you found out."

"You were kind of busy," Jane said, tossing the covers

149

back to sit up on the mattress. Putting her feet on the floor, she slid out of bed and moved carefully to the bathroom where she shut the door behind her.

She leaned back against the door, staring at her reflection in the mirror. She looked like crap. Her hair was limp and dull, her face was white as a sheet, and her nightgown hung on her toothin body.

She used the bathroom before running a brush through her hair. Reluctantly opening the door, she reentered her bedroom to find it empty. Staring in dismay at her bedroom clock, she went to her closet to pull out some clothes.

"What in the fuck are you doing?" Cade asked from the doorway.

"I'm two hours late for work."

"No, you're not. Get back in bed. Crazy Bitch called in and told them you're sick." Cade placed the tray he was holding down on her nightstand.

Jane walked back to the bed, sitting down before she fluffed up her pillows so she could lean back against the headboard. After Cade placed the tray of food on her lap, she stared down at the huge plate.

"I can't eat all of this," she protested.

"You're going to eat it all. I'm not leaving until you do."

Jane picked up her fork, shoveling the egg into her mouth, while Cade sat down on the bed next to her and watched her eat.

"The day you left your phone in my room and I didn't know it, I tried calling you several times. You told me you would come back to the clubhouse in a few hours, and when you didn't show and my calls weren't answered, I began to get mad. I know it was juvenile, but it didn't make me any less angry. When you showed up and caught me with Demie, I felt like shit, but then I pushed you away even though I wanted you so badly. You had left me once already at the hotel in Corpus Christi, and when I couldn't reach you, my pride took a hit. It seemed like I was always the one chasing after you. Stupid, yeah?"

Jane remained silent, eating her food, wishing he would just leave.

"I couldn't get a decent night's sleep after you left Corpus Christi. I thought that, after I fucked you, wanting you would ease up. It didn't. It only became worse.

"Every morning, when I woke up with a different woman next to me, I intended to get on my bike and leave town, just like I've left every other place I've stopped in. But I couldn't this time, because I would be leaving you behind. Even though I knew I had screwed up what was between us, I kept thinking about you, hoping to be with you again."

Jane set her fork down on her empty plate. "I'm finished. Will you go now?"

Cade took the tray and set it down on the nightstand. "I'll go, but I'll be back tonight. Crazy Bitch said your new favorite restaurant is the steakhouse. I'll bring you dinner." Cade stood up, putting out a hand to cup her cheek. "I'm sorry about the baby."

"Go away, Cade. Please, just go away. I don't need this right now."

"I know you don't, but I'll be back, anyway. The doctor told Crazy Bitch you need to gain at least fifteen pounds, and I'm going to make sure you do. Then, when you're healthy enough, I'm going to put another baby in you."

Jane picked up the tray sitting next to her and threw it at him. "You can't replace what I lost!" she cried out. "It's not like going out and getting a new puppy when the old one dies."

"No, it isn't," he said hoarsely. "But it will be a part of you and me, the beginning of the family I intend to have with you." He picked up the scattered dishes, placing them back on the tray before going to the door, where he stared back at her mercilessly as she sat crying.

Opening the door, he went out and reached back for

the handle. "By the way, I called your boss at Popeye's and told her you quit, and if she gave you your job back, I would make sure the brothers came to eat there for all their meals."

He barely managed to shut the door before her bedside clock crashed against it.

Chapter Twenty-three

Jane was sitting on the couch, playing with her cat, when Cade knocked on the door later that day.

"Don't open it," Jane told Crazy Bitch.

Her friend went to the door to look out the peephole. "The dude is standing outside with bags of food."

"I don't care. Don't—" Crazy Bitch didn't wait to listen to the rest of her sentence. She just opened the door.

"Give me the bags and get lost." Crazy Bitch blocked the doorway.

Jane heard Cade's determined voice and knew Crazy Bitch wasn't going to win this battle.

"I brought enough for all of us. Either I come in, or I take the bags with me."

"Fuck." Crazy Bitch moved back from the doorway, letting him inside.

"Are you feeling better?" Cade asked when he saw Jane

sitting on the couch.

Jane didn't answer him, still angry about losing her job at Popeye's.

Cade simply grinned and set the two large bags on the coffee table in front of her. As he reached inside the bag and pulled out an aluminum foil covered bread roll, Jane couldn't help herself. She started salivating at the smells coming from the bag.

"I'll get us some plates," Crazy Bitch said as she went to the kitchen.

Cade sat down next to Jane. She was about to warn him yet wasn't given a chance.

"What the hell?" the cat was swatting at Cade's arm.

"That's Manson. Get used to him." Crazy Bitch came back in and pulled a chair closer to the coffee table. She then took out three round aluminum trays and gave one each to Jane and Cade before she took the last one for herself.

Not able to resist the temptation any longer, Jane took off the cardboard top and stared down at the thick T-bone and mashed potatoes with asparagus.

"I hate asparagus," she told him, about to put the offending vegetable on Crazy Bitch's plate.

"Eat it. It's good for you," Cade said, popping a stalk of it in his own mouth.

"I hate it."

After Cade dropped a dollop of butter on the vegetable she hated, Jane looked at it for a second. The butter did make it seem more appetizing. She lifted one to her mouth and took a small bite, chewing it thoughtfully before eating the rest of it. Cade smiled, eating the rest of his while Jane ignored him.

Cade had to repeatedly smack the cat away from him, finally giving up and ignoring it.

"You can have him if you want him." Cade almost choked on a bite of his steak at Crazy Bitch's offer. "I'll even pack his litter box and cat food to the clubhouse for you."

"No, thanks," Cade managed to get out.

"He's free. You can take him with you tonight."

"Crazy Bitch, that's my cat," Jane said, laughing at Cade's expression.

"No, he's not. He's Bailey's. You got stuck with him when she wanted to put him down."

"He's mine now. He didn't like Bailey, but he likes me," Jane lied.

"That mean fucker don't like anyone, and if he doesn't quit shedding, I'm going to cough up a hairball."

Jane finished eating, curling her legs under her on the couch. She petted her cat, ignoring the constant swatting.

After they all were finished eating, Cade dumped the trash into the empty bags while Crazy Bitch took the dirty plates to the kitchen.

"I thought we could watch some television, if you're not too tired," Cade suggested.

Jane stood up from the couch, barely holding on to her squirming cat. "You can watch it with Crazy Bitch. I'm going back to bed. I have to be up early for work in the morning." Without giving him a chance to say anything, she went into her bedroom and closed the door.

Jane was determined not to give him another chance. He had been the one who decided he didn't want her. Just because he was feeling bad she'd had a miscarriage was no reason to begin a relationship that wasn't going to last.

Cade was never going to be happy in Jamestown, and she wasn't going to spend the rest of her life pining for a man she couldn't have like her mother. Jane was convinced she would get over him. After all, they'd had sex only one time. How hard could it be?

Jane sat down on her bed glumly, hearing Cade and Crazy Bitch's voices from the other room. Maybe it wasn't going to be as easy as she'd thought.

* * *

Jane rushed out her door, not wanting to keep Rock

waiting. Killyama used to drive her to work, but Rock had taken over during the last two weeks. She came down her apartment stairs, seeing Cade sitting there, instead.

"Why are you here?"

"Rock couldn't find his keys."

Jane stared at Cade angrily.

"Get on. I'll drive you to work."

Jane looked down at her watch. She didn't have time to argue with him; as a result, she got on behind him and clutched his waist as he pulled out of the parking lot.

Her apartment wasn't far from the hospital; Jane could have walked it if she had to. In fact, she had done so many times. However, the early morning was dark, and she had promised her friends never to walk this early.

He swung into a fast food restaurant, going through the drive-thru and ordering an oatmeal and orange juice. At the window, he told her to take the bag.

"Make sure you eat it before it gets cold."

"I hate oatmeal."

He took off again, ignoring her words while Jane sat fuming. If he hadn't been driving, she would have dumped the contents of the bag over his head.

As soon as he came to a stop in front of the hospital, she climbed off.

"I don't need you to take care of me. I've taken care of myself since I was sixteen."

"Eat your breakfast. You can bitch at me later." With that, he took off, leaving her standing in the parking lot.

She went inside the building, going to her small cubicle. She had a few minutes until they would start sending patients back to be checked in; therefore, she opened the orange juice and drank it as she opened the oatmeal.

When she was younger, she had loved oatmeal, dumping copious amounts of sugar into the sticky goo. Even now, she would fix herself a bowl whenever she needed a warm comfort food. She had told him she hated oatmeal to be annoying. If he wanted to treat her like a child, then she would act like one. She didn't need him to act all protective and caring when she knew it was all only an act to salve his conscience.

However, if he kept feeding her like this, she just might let him waste his time.

* * *

"It's been two months. How long are you going to keep torturing the bastard?" Sex Piston asked as Jane danced with Crazy Bitch.

She hadn't felt this good in a long time. She had gained weight, felt stronger, and mentally, she was finally beginning to be in a good place again. She refused to admit it was because of the attention Cade was showing her.

She never knew if Rock or Cade would be the one to show up to take her to and from work. Rock had steadily become a good friend of hers, and she would have jumped him long before now, but something had held her back from beginning a relationship with him. And that something was Cade.

"I can't stand the fucker, but it's starting to get nasty between those two. You need to cut one of them loose," Killyama stated as she danced with T.A.

"I've tried to get rid of Cade, but he won't listen. As soon as Stud gets his bike done, he'll take off."

"Stud says it should be done in about two months."

"Then he'll be gone before Christmas. Merry Christmas to me." Jane lowered her eyes to the dance floor, not letting her friends see the hopelessness in her eyes.

"I need a beer." Crazy Bitch fanned herself in the stuffy room.

"Me, too," Sex Piston seconded.

"I'll grab us all one," Jane offered, leaving her friends on the dance floor.

Deciding to use the restroom first, she veered in that direction. As she passed the doorway that led to the men's bedrooms, she saw Demie standing outside Cade's bedroom, talking to him. She caught Jane staring at her.

"What you staring at, bitch?" Demie snapped.

Jane started to walk off, ignoring her harsh words, but then anger flooded through her. She had been right not to take Cade's attention seriously.

Jane turned around and snapped, "Fuck off!"

"What did you say to me?" Demie turned to face her.

"You too stupid to understand what I said?" Jane lost her temper, moving farther down the hall, closer to her and Cade, who was watching the building argument.

"You're being brave tonight without your friends at your back. They must be within yelling distance, or you wouldn't be up in my face."

"I'm in your face because, every time you see me, you have something smart to say to me, and I'm sick of it."

"That makes us even because I'm sick of everyone feeling sorry for you and walking on egg-shells." As soon as the words had left Demie's mouth, she found herself flattened against the wall with Cade's hand on her throat.

"Don't ever talk that way to her again. If you're pissed at me, take it out on me, not her. I told you two months ago that I didn't want what you were begging to give. I've tried to be nice about it, but now I'm warning you to not fucking open your mouth to my woman again. You understand me?"

"Yes," Demie managed to get out.

"Good." Cade released her, and she took off down the hall, brushing past Jane.

"You weren't going to have sex with her?"

"I don't want another woman." Cade reached out to cup her cheek.

"I can't let you hurt me again."

"I won't." His thumb traced her bottom lip.

"I don't trust you."

Cade leaned forward, gently touching her lips with his. His hand cupped the back of her neck as he walked backward into his bedroom. Shutting the door, he pressed her back against it.

"Give me another chance."

"No. I'm not going to give you another chance to hurt me. If we do this, it's going to be what it is—just sex," Jane said, the words stripping her soul away. "Leave town when you want. Do what you want. I'm not going to expect a damn thing from you, Cade."

Cade felt her words as if they were flicks of a whip against his skin. She was emotionally distancing herself from him.

Tracing her lips with his tongue, he then parted them, thrusting inside. The faint moan she gave as he drew her closer to his body revealed the lie of her trying to remain aloof. Her tongue dueled with his, searching his mouth in turn, her passion showing her hunger for him. When Cade gave her the control she was searching for, he felt her hands run over his chest, going to the snap of his jeans and unzipping them.

Cade nipped at her neck before breaking the kiss to take off her T-shirt. His hand went for the little cherry nipples he had fantasized about for the last six months. He groaned as their sweet taste filled his mouth.

"No one tastes like you." Cade's hand went to her hips, sliding down her pants. Kneeling in front of her, he took off her boots and pants before nuzzling her smooth stomach. "You taste like candy. I'm going to make you melt in my mouth." Cade parted her thighs, placing one over his shoulder as she braced herself against the door.

"Cade...what I thought we had that night was special, it's gone I don't feel that way anymore."

"Just because a rose looses a few petals, doesn't mean it isn't still beautiful."

His tongue slid between the lips of her pussy, going back and forth, rubbing her clit. Her hands clutched his shoulders as he felt the fine tremors of her climax.

He gave a short laugh. "You were hungry, weren't you?" Cade looked up to see her face turn bright red.

He stood, picking her up, and her legs wrapped around

his waist. Cade turned to his bed, placing her on the soft mattress, where he stared at her hungrily as he took off his boots and jeans before ripping off his T-shirt. When his hands returned to her thighs, she stopped him.

"Get a condom. I'm not fucking you without one."

Cade didn't argue with her. Opening the drawer of his nightstand, he grabbed one. A minute later, he was slipping between her warm thighs.

"You know what I love about fucking you?" He slid his dick into her welcoming wetness, nudging his cock into her opening. "You don't take forever to warm up. Most women want twenty minutes of foreplay, and then two for fucking."

"Why waste my appetite on an appetizer when I can have dinner, instead?"

Cade caught the tip of her nipple in his mouth as he thrust his length fully inside her. "You can fight how you feel about me all you want, but your pussy is telling me all I need to know."

"Women fuck men all the time that they don't care about," Jane gasped.

Cade tilted her hips upwards, driving his cock into her more forcefully. Her body recognized her feelings even as her mind fought them.

"Then why were you a virgin the first time I fucked you? Why haven't you fucked Rock? Because you only wanted me, just like I only want you."

"No." Jane shook her head back and forth on the pillow, denying his words.

"Yes, Jane. I've quit running from it, and you will, too." His mouth dropped to her, driving his point home by driving her passion higher, making her become so lost the only way she could find herself again was to cling to him as their bodies moved together. Her whimpers of release had him fucking her faster as his own climax tore through his cock.

Jane turned her head, taking her mouth away. "You

done?"

Cade raised his head, staring at the woman who refused to look at him. "Yeah..."

"Then get off." She pushed at his shoulders.

As soon as he moved, she slid out of the bed and picked her clothes up off the floor before going to the bathroom. She came out a few minutes later, dressed again.

"Where are you going?"

"Back outside." She combed her fingers through her hair, smoothing it out.

"I thought...?"

"What did you think? That I'd lie here and let you fuck me all night like you did the other bitches in the club? No, thank you. I need to go get the girls their beers." Jane went out the door, slamming it shut behind her, ignoring the words he said in warning.

"Run, Jane, but when you get tired, I'll still be here. I'm not going anywhere."

Chapter Twenty-four

Jane sat on a bale of hay as she watched her friends lead Sex Piston's kids through the field to pick out pumpkins. Her youngest was dressed in blue jeans overalls, and Jane's lips twitched at the little Harley motorcycle jacket he was wearing. The little boy was going to be gorgeous when he grew up. She didn't envy Sex Piston having to deal with all his girlfriends.

Jane's smile slipped and disappeared as Lily came into view. She was holding Chance, one of her sister Beth's twins. Her baby bump was barely noticeable, and she glowed with health and happiness. T.A. came up to her, snagging the child away, and Lily laughed, brushing her wind-swept black hair away from her face. Jane saw her then go inside the store attached to the pumpkin patch.

Jane dug her boot into the dirt when she noticed Cade sitting on his motorcycle, talking to Stud and Dozer, his serious eyes keeping her within sight. Cade was constantly where he could watch Jane. Sometimes, she wondered why; other times, she ignored it, pretending he wasn't there.

She was falling for him again, and she didn't know how to stop what was happening. It was like standing on the edge of a cliff, knowing you were going to die if you jumped, but you did it anyway for the thrill of adrenaline that jumping would bring. Every time she let him lure her to his bed, she knew she would be jumping headfirst over that cliff. She couldn't resist the feelings he gave her, though.

Lily came out of the store carrying two cups. Smiling, she headed toward her, and Jane scooted over on the hay bale to make room.

"You looked like you were cold. I thought this would warm us up."

Once Lily handed her a warm cup of apple cider, Jane took a sip, enjoying the warmth and cinnamon taste. "Thank you."

"You're welcome. The kids are all growing so fast." Jane caught the faint hint of sadness in Lily's voice.

"Thank goodness. I'm on everyone's speed dial for babysitting. How is Cash recovering from his accident?"

"He's been moved to a rehabilitation center. He's doing better. Shade says he's getting stronger every day."

"It won't be long before he gets out and makes up for lost time with the women in Treepoint," Jane wisecracked.

Lily laughed, tilting her head toward Cade. "Your boyfriend seems nice."

"He's not my boyfriend," Jane denied.

"Does he know that?" Lily teased. "He reminds me of Shade. He never lets me out of his sight, either."

"He's nothing like Shade. Shade loves you. Everyone knew how he felt about you before you did. Cade doesn't care about me. He just feels guilty and trapped."

Lily went quiet, her eyes gazing back at Jane in

compassion, before she said, "I didn't see it, and maybe you don't, either. Sex Piston told me about your loss. I'm really sorry."

Jane blinked back tears, turning away from Lily. She was still heartsick over losing her baby. When she had found out she was pregnant, she hadn't been upset; she had been overjoyed. She wanted a family so badly, and the tiny baby was going to be the beginning of one. After she had lost the baby, she felt all alone again.

"I didn't mean to bring up something so painful."

"It's all right."

"No, it's not. You looked so sad sitting here, and I wanted to cheer you up, not make it worse." Lily started to get to her feet.

"Don't go. It really wasn't anything you said. It's me." Jane licked her dry lips. "I was sitting here, watching you, and I'm so jealous I can't stand it. I see you looking absolutely beautiful and healthy, pregnant with your baby, while I lost mine." Jane felt the tears sliding down her cheeks, unable to help herself.

Lily enfolded Jane in her arms.

"I know I should be getting over it since I was only two months along, but I had already picked out names, and I was pestering Crazy Bitch to take me shopping for a crib. I love babies. I've always wanted a lot, and I didn't miss Cade as much when I felt his baby in me." Jane didn't know why she was spilling all her baggage onto Lily, who sat listening as she held her, letting her cry on her shoulder. She had held back with her friends, but Lily's gentleness had loosened the tight grip of grief she had bottled up inside of her.

After several minutes, she managed to gather her shattered control.

Lily released her, taking her hand. "There's no need to be jealous." She placed Jane's hand on her stomach, and Jane caught her breath at the feel of the tightness of her growing womb. "We can share. I know nothing will replace the one you lost, but when you want one to hug or love, you can hold this one. He needs a godmother," Lily said hesitantly.

She was offering her a gift to share a child. Not to replace hers, but to fill an aching void that would help her heal.

"I would be honored."

"That's settled, then." She looked toward Cade before dropping her voice. "Cade is throwing me dirty looks. He thinks I've upset you."

Jane smiled at Lily. The gentle woman wasn't capable of hurting anyone. She always went out of her way to be friendly and helpful.

Shade appeared at Cade's side, joining in the conversation the men were having. Both men stood facing their women.

"See, I told you they're alike," Lily teased then grew serious. "I didn't want to see that Shade cared about me, because I was too scared. Maybe you are, too. Shade helped me through my fears. If you let him, Cade could help you through yours, too. It's much better than trying to do it alone."

"I'm tired of being alone. I want someone to want me," Jane confessed. "I always feel as if I'm imposing on everyone, since I don't have a car because my mom has a knack for stealing them and selling them for drugs. You know, I bought her four cell phones, and she kept each one for a couple of days before they disappeared. Sex Piston, Killyama, T.A., and Crazy Bitch all look out for me, but I sometimes feel like the weakest link."

"You're not their weakest link; you're the link that holds the chain together. Those women love you. Don't ever doubt that."

"I won't." Jane gave her the first genuine smile she'd had in a long time.

"Good. Now I'm going to get my husband and sneak off to that barn over there. I've always wanted to make out in a haystack." Lily stood, picking up their now empty cups to throw away before going to her husband.

Jane released a deep breath, standing up. She brushed down her jeans, thinking Lily wasn't the only one who intended to find a haystack.

* * *

"Ready?" Cade asked impatiently.

"I'm hurrying." Jane wiggled her butt into a short leather skirt then pulled on a bright red sweater. "How do I look?"

"All Christmassy."

Jane twirled. "That's what I was going for."

The club was having their annual Christmas party at the clubhouse. Instead of the members giving each other presents, everyone coming was supposed to bring a toy to be donated.

"I would prefer it if you dressed as one of Santa's helpers," Cade suggested with a leer.

"Be good, and I'll give you a present when we come back here tonight," Jane teased.

Cade had been spending a lot of time with her, catering to her every need. The only things keeping her from being spoiled from all the attention were the reasons she thought he was giving it to her. They had never discussed the tiny baby they had created and lost. In some ways, it had drawn him to her, while it had pushed her away from him. She couldn't forgive how he had been with other women in the clubhouse after his night with her, nor had he regained her trust. She didn't know if he ever would, despite that she enjoyed spending time with him, getting to know him better, and learning he had never had much of a family life. It was ironic. She wanted a loving family and home to replace the one she had never had, whereas Cade ran from the thought of a family, too wary of the pain his own had inflicted.

"We're not staying here tonight; we're staying at the club. I need to get away from Crazy Bitch and that cat. I don't know which of them is worse. At least the fucking cat sleeps a lot."

"That's not nice."

"It's the truth," Cade stated, handing her the black jacket she had laid on the bed. "Let's go."

They went into the living room where several brightly colored Christmas presents were wrapped. Killyama was already blowing her horn outside.

"Does she have to do that?" Cade asked impatiently as he picked up several of the packages. Jane also picked up several to take herself.

"Take those on down and tell her I'm coming." Crazy Bitch came into the room, looking fabulous in a green leather top with black leggings.

Jane and Cade packed the presents down the steps to Killyama's car, and then Jane climbed into the backseat. Cade was going to follow on his motorcycle.

Crazy Bitch put the remaining presents in the trunk, slamming it closed before she climbed into the front seat next to Killyama.

"Did you buy out the store?" Killyama asked as she drove out of the parking lot.

"Almost," Jane conceded. She had bought more than she had originally intended.

As they drove past the street that Jane's mother lived on, she turned her head to look toward the apartment complex. Blue lights were flashing outside her mother's building, which was divided into four apartments.

"Wait! Killyama, go to Mom's house. The cops are out front." Jane felt the beginning of panic as Killyama quickly took a sharp left.

Jane jumped out of the car, running toward her mother. The police were walking her out in handcuffs. She was kicking out at the officers as they tried to push her toward the patrol car.

"Step back." Another officer by the police car blocked her from getting closer to her mother.

"That's my mother. What happened?"

"She sold crack to an undercover police officer."

Her mother was still resisting the officers, screaming profanities. Her brown hair looked like it hadn't been brushed since the last time Jane had seen her, which had been last week, and she was wearing a small pair of shorts that looked like they belonged to a teenager. In fact, Jane thought they were a pair of shorts she had worn in middle school. She also had on a T-shirt with no bra. It wasn't a pretty sight.

"She's been selling drugs to the kids in the neighborhood for a while now. We were finally able to catch her an hour ago."

Jane took a step away from her mother, coming up against Cade, whose arm went around her waist in support. She had forgotten he had been following them.

"Don't just stand there, call a lawyer. That stuck-up sister of Sex Piston's is a lawyer, isn't she? Call her. Tell her these sons of bitches are violating my civil liberties. I was in my own home watching TV." Jane easily recognized the signs of her mother being high. "Get busy, you good for nothing slut. You better get me out of jail in an hour, or I'm going to smack the shit out of you."

Jane merely stood there as the police finally managed to shove her mother into the police car where she began using her feet to kick at the window. She stared coldly at her mother, realizing the woman was never going to change. Each time Jane went to visit her and gave her money, her mother would promise to be different.

Jane had paid for three trips to different rehabilitation centers, each making the promise to help her mother. However, they had all failed, just like her own daughter had failed because, ultimately, the woman didn't want to be helped.

"I'll call Sex Piston." Killyama pulled out her cell phone.

"Don't bother. Let's get to the party. We're already

late." Jane didn't watch the patrol cars as they drove away.

"You sure?"

"I'm sure." Jane got back in the car. Killyama and Crazy Bitch both gave her curious looks as they also climbed back in, as well.

The ride to the clubhouse was short, and the parking lot was filled with bikes by the time they arrived. Cade came up to her as soon as she got out of the car.

"I could call a lawyer. I know he could—"

"Leave it alone, Cade. Maybe jail time can do what I couldn't, but. I'm not going to think about that tonight. It's three weeks until Christmas, and I want to have some fun. Can you help me with that?"

"Darlin', I can give you all the fun you can handle."

Chapter Twenty-five

Cade grinned as he watched the four women dancing, commanding everyone's attention.

"They're something else, aren't they?" A man Cade hadn't seen before stood next to him, drinking a beer. "I'm Skulls, former President of the Destructors." When the man reached out his hand, Cade shook it.

"You're Sex Piston's father?"

"Guilty." Her father laughed. "She been busting your balls?"

"A couple of times," Cade admitted.

"Only a couple? Hell, she must like you." The old man hit him on his back, knocking him forward against the bar.

"Which one's your old lady?"

"How do you know one of them is mine?"

The man gave a sudden burst of laughter. "From the way you're glaring at all the brothers thinking of approaching them. Stud's on the other side of the bar doing the same fucking thing."

"Jane."

"Jane?"

"Fat Louise," Cade said through gritted teeth. He was fast learning where Sex Piston had inherited her abrasive personality from.

"Aw, you're a lucky man. She's a sweet girl. Sometimes." He took a swig of his beer. "You met that cat of hers yet?"

"Yes, I have," Cade said grimly.

"I need some extra money for Christmas; want me to get rid of it for you?"

Was the man offering to kill Jane's cat for him? Cade took a drink of his own beer, tempted by the thought. "No, thanks. I kinda like it," he lied.

"You fucking liar. No one likes that crazy motherfucker. But I can respect a man who will lie to protect his woman's feelings. Been doing that my whole married life. If my wife invites you over to dinner, run. She can't cook for shit." He leaned heavily against the bar. Sex Piston's father was drunk off his ass. "Didn't catch your name?"

"Cade."

"What kind of name is that?"

"I was born with it."

"The brothers ain't given you a nickname yet?"

"Other than, 'hey asshole,' no, they haven't."

"They call him Traveler," Stud said, taking a seat next to his father-in-law.

"Why they call him that?"

"Because they know he's not here to stay," Stud answered. "He's waiting for me to finish building his bike."

"I thought you finished that bike a week ago."

"I did," Stud answered, meeting Cade's eyes. "I was trying to get him to stay around until after Christmas."

"You shouldn't hold the man up if he wants to leave," Skulls reproached Stud.

"You can give me the bike. I'm not going anywhere," Cade told Stud. "I'm done traveling. I've gotten weak. The whole time I was moving from town to town and fucking woman after woman, I thought I was happy." His eyes went around the clubroom, looking at the men he had grown close to over the past few months. His eyes stopped on Jane.

"When I met Jane, I was attracted to her. I planned to fuck her before we left Corpus, but she took off before I could. When I came to Jamestown, I thought I'd fuck her then leave town." He gave a wry smile. "How I felt about her scared the shit out of me, so I fucked it up. I couldn't admit even to myself how much I cared until Sex Piston let it spill about the baby." Cade's voice went hoarse. "Never thought I wanted a woman and kid until I lost them both. I won't be making that mistake ever again. Everyone at this fucking clubhouse has become my family, despite me not wanting one. I might not have been born into the family I wanted, but one day, I'll die in one that was everything I could ever want."

Stud nodded his head. "Stop by the garage and pick it up tomorrow."

Cade grinned. "Looking forward to it."

"What are those girls doing now?"

Cade and Stud both looked toward the dance floor to see Jane and Demie fighting. Sex Piston, Killyama, T.A., and Crazy Bitch were daring anyone to interfere.

When Cade reached the dance floor, Jane had Demie on the floor with her hands buried in her hair. One of her earrings was lying on the floor next to her with a piece of the skin still attached.

"I told you not to bother me. Maybe now you will listen!"

Cade wrapped his arms around Jane, lifting her off Demie.

"What in the hell happened?" Stud yelled.

"Stupid bitch kept taunting Fat Louise about fucking Cade. Said he knocked her up, too!" Sex Piston snarled at the woman trying to get to her feet.

"He did! I'm three months pregnant!" Demie yelled.

Fury hit Cade at Demie's accusation. "You're lying, and you know it."

"Don't touch me." Jane tried to get away from Cade, but he held on to her.

He jerked her off the dance floor, taking her to his room despite her flailing arms as she tried to get away. Cade managed to get his door open then pushed her inside before shutting the door behind him.

"You bastard! Did you know?" Cade saw the hurt in her eyes.

Battling back his own anger from her not believing him, Cade told her grimly, "I did not get her pregnant. I haven't touched her since I started seeing you again."

"Did you use a condom with her?" Jane shrieked at him.

"Yes. I haven't fucked anyone but you without a condom."

"Thank God I made you use one after that one night." While Jane walked agitatedly around the room in circles, Cade used the time to diffuse his own anger, leaning back against the door.

"Jane, if she's pregnant, I'm telling you, it's not mine."

Jane came to a standstill, and Cade swallowed hard at the heartbreak on her face.

"You could be. You had sex with her."

"Any brother here could be the baby's father. Except Stud," Cade clarified.

"You didn't know I was pregnant until it was too late, and my baby was gone." Jane went to her knees on the floor, burying her face in her hands.

"Our baby." Cade knelt beside her, holding her close as sobs tore through her body. His own eyes watered. "Do you really think that, after losing one baby, I would ever deny a child that was mine?"

Jane looked up at him and saw his anguish at losing that fragile life. She had needed to know he cared, that he, too, had wanted to see their child grow into adulthood. To know that he had experienced the same feelings of loss she had suffered.

"There's something inside of me that's broken, and I can't fix it."

"We can fix it together, you don't have to do it alone." Cade promised.

"What's broken can't be pieced together again." She cried out, her arms holding her stomach as she rocked back and forth.

"No, but it can be made into something new, something stronger, that can't be broken."

"All the pieces aren't there anymore." He cupped her cheek with the palm of his hand, his thumb wiping away her tears.

"The strong always survives." Cade told her about his childhood, being forced to beg for money. It wasn't an easy thing for a man to confess to a woman he loved. Jane's heart melted taking away the last barricade she had placed to protect herself from him.

Jane's arms circled his neck, and she hungrily kissed his mouth with all the desire she had been holding back. Cade eagerly took control, parting her lips to give her the passion she was searching for.

She brought her hands to his T-shirt, pulling it off. After she went to his jeans, unsnapping them, she took her mouth away from his to lick his nipple. Cade groaned, feeling the wildness emanating from Jane. She licked his other nipple until it was a tight bead before seductively looking up at him beneath lowered lashes.

"I'm jealous-natured," she confessed, giving him a hard shove backward.

Cade landed on the floor with her above him. She

traced his nipples with the tip of a finger before her hand moved downward, reaching inside his open jeans to pull out his cock.

Some men might not appreciate an aggressive woman; however, Cade didn't have that problem.

His hips lifted off the floor as Jane leaned down over him, taking his cock into her mouth.

"No foreplay?" he teased.

Jane let his cock slip from her mouth. "I can do foreplay." She flicked her tongue against the head of his dick.

His hand went to the back of her head, pushing her back down. "Fuck foreplay. Suck my dick."

Jane parted her lips as he thrust upward, burying his cock in her warm mouth. She didn't take her eyes off his face as she sucked him down her throat, watching his reaction as she swallowed while using her tongue to rub the underside of his cock. Her hand delved farther inside his jeans until she was cupping his balls, massaging them with her fingers in a way that sent lightning bolts through his nuts.

"Darlin', after I come, I'm going to suck on your clit until you come in my mouth. Then I'm going to fuck you until you beg for mercy," Cade promised between gasping breaths. God, he was glad the brothers couldn't hear him, because he was making noises like a girl.

Jane swallowed again, using her tongue to press his cock to the roof of her mouth. Cade shouted as he came, holding her head to him.

After his cock quit jerking, she took her mouth away, and he rolled over on the floor, tugging at her until she tumbled backwards. Flipping her skirt to her waist, he tore off her panties seconds before his mouth went down on her. She was already wet.

Cade's tongue went to her clit, finding the sensitive bud red and swollen. Sucking it into his mouth, he gently bit down, and Jane screamed in pleasure.

Cade then pulled away to reach into his back pocket for a condom. He spread her legs wider, not giving her time to catch her breath, before he plunged inside her to the hilt and began to steadily thrust, building her passion again.

"That bitch didn't get pregnant by me. My sperm has better sense than finding a home in her pussy." His mouth found hers. "They were in heaven when I put my dick in you." Cade jerked her hips up to his, burrowing farther with each stroke. "This daddy is going to love the mother of his children."

Jane's eyes widened as she stared up at him. "Are you saying…?"

"I'm saying only one woman is ever going to know what it's like having my seed in her belly, and that's you. I love you, Jane."

Her face softened with a gentle glow. "I love you, too."

"You sure about that? I'm not going to let you take it back," Cade threatened as he felt her pussy grip his cock until he couldn't hold back his own climax. He buried his face in her shoulder, and her hands went to his hair, tugging his head up until their eyes met.

"I'm a bitch. I don't give up anything that's mine, either."

Chapter Twenty-six

Jane practically skipped to the hospital doors as soon as she clocked out. Killyama was going to the clubhouse; as a result, she had offered to pick Jane up from work. Jane had texted Cade, but he hadn't replied. She was sure he was too busy riding his new toy he had been planning to pick up from Stud's garage today.

Killyama threw her a sour look at the beaming smile Jane gave her once she was seated in the car next to her.

"Work was great today. Ms. Garber said she was going to put me in for a raise."

"That's great," Killyama responded, turning onto the road.

"I'm going to get Cade to take me to the Taco Hut to celebrate."

Killyama made a gagging noise.

"What's wrong?"

"All you ever talk about anymore is that man. It makes me want to vomit rainbows and shit gummy bears," she said snidely.

"You're just jealous you aren't getting any." Jane stuck out her tongue, not letting her friend dampen her mood.

"It sure as fuck isn't from lack of trying. Every time I look at a dude, they take off running."

Jane rolled her eyes. "I wonder why."

"What the hell does that mean?" Killyama snapped as she turned into the clubhouse.

"It means that you fucking shame them. Everyone knows you gave Train hell because he didn't perform well, and they don't want the same said about them. Men are sensitive about things like that."

"I didn't say he had a small dick." She shrugged. "It just would have been better if he had lasted longer."

"His dick was probably too scared. I'm surprised he was even able to get it up." She laughed, dodging Killyama's mock threatening fist.

Jumping out of the car, she looked around the parking lot, surprised Cade wasn't outside with his new bike. She looked up and down the road, searching for him.

Killyama held the door to the clubhouse open for her. "Coming?"

"Yeah." Jane went inside where there were only a few brothers hanging out and saw Stud sitting at a table with Sex Piston, Crazy Bitch, and T.A.

"What's up?" she asked as she drew nearer to the table. By the looks on their faces, it wasn't good news.

"Have a seat," Sex Piston said, pulling out a chair.

Jane stood still. "Tell me."

Stud's voice broke the silence at the table. "Cade's gone. When I called to see why he hadn't been in to pick up his bike, Rock went in his room to look. All his things are gone. When I came in, I checked, too. He just left. No word. No note."

Jane stood numbly. Sex Piston reached out to take her

hand, and Jane gripped it tightly, determined not to break down in front of everyone.

"You all expected it, didn't you?"

Her friends couldn't meet her eyes.

"He didn't take his new bike?"

"No." Stud's grim voice had her giving him a weak smile.

"Then he must be coming back." Jane tried to give herself hope. He had told her last night he loved her, and why would he tell her that if it wasn't true? "He'll be back," Jane said more firmly.

"You're right; he'll be back." Sex Piston tried to sound more upbeat, although Jane could tell none of them believed it.

"I'm getting a raise," Jane told the group then listened to their forced congratulations.

"Want to go to the Taco Hut? I was going to get Cade to go, but…"

"Sounds good. I'll even pay," Crazy Bitch said.

As her friends all stood, ready to leave, Jane pushed her hurt back. She would deal with it later when she was in her bedroom alone. Right now, she needed to be with the women who were her sisters in every way except blood. That would make the hurt bearable because, unlike everyone else who swore they loved her, they were always by her side.

* * *

"We're almost ready to eat," T.A. said as she passed by with another casserole dish in her hands.

Jane stared at the huge dinner laid out at the clubhouse. They had pulled all the tables together to make a long one, and a huge, twenty-five pound turkey took the place of honor at the head of the table.

"I think I'm going to go back to the apartment," she told Crazy Bitch, who was balancing several bottles of cheap wine.

"Don't go. Stay."

"You can bring me a plate of leftovers." Her hunger was nonexistent, but she would force herself to eat something when Crazy Bitch came home later. She hadn't had much of an appetite for the last three weeks that Cade had been gone.

Jane shrugged into her coat, going to the door.

"It's snowing. You want me to drive you?" Crazy Bitch offered.

"No, my car has four-wheel drive. I'll be fine." With her mom still in jail, Jane had bought herself a new car. Stud had offered to go with her to buy it, yet she had refused, wanting to do it on her own.

Cade had left her with a broken heart; however, he had made her more confident during the time they had been together. She didn't need to lean so heavily on her friends anymore. They might still be adjusting to her newfound independence, but they were enjoying the benefits of riding in a car with a functioning heater.

Outside, the snow was falling heavily. Jane tilted her head back, feeling the snowflakes land on her cheeks, when the sound of a bike's motor resonated in the distance.

Jane's eyes went to the road, seeing a lone biker drive into the lot, barely managing to keep his motorcycle from sliding. Jane recognized him through the snow, and his haggard appearance brought an unwanted lump to her throat.

Cade climbed off his bike and began to walk toward the clubhouse yet came to an abrupt stop when he saw her.

Jane stood still for a heartbeat then took off running toward him, almost slipping in the snow before she was caught up in his arms.

"You came back. You came back!" Her tears mixed with the snow.

"Of course I came back. I said I would."

"I didn't know. You left without a word…"

"What are you talking about? I left a fucking note in my room."

"No one found it. It doesn't matter now. All that matters is that you're back."

"It does matter, Jane. I wouldn't have left without telling you why."

"All I care about is that you're here now. I understand that you wanted some time to think—"

Cade cut her off. "Jane, let's go to my room. I have something to tell you."

Was he going to leave again? Had he come back only to pick up his bike and tell her it was over?

When Jane followed him inside the clubhouse, everyone at the table went quiet as they saw Cade. Sex Piston and Killyama both flung back their chairs.

"I'm going to talk to Jane first, and then I'll explain to the rest of you. But she deserves to hear it alone and in private." Cade looked at Stud. "My old room still open?"

Stud took a moment before answering, "Always, brother. This is your home as long as you want it." Stud ignored his wife's gasp. "Skulls, quick hogging the ham and pass it here."

Cade took Jane's cold hand, leading her to his bedroom. The short walk didn't last long enough for Jane, who was already preparing herself for his goodbye.

He shut the door to the bedroom before releasing her hand.

"Let's sit down." Cade's gruff voice had her following his direction.

Once she took off her coat, laying it on the chair before sitting stiffly on the bed, Cade sat down next to her on the bed, placing his arm around her. "Darlin', I have some bad news."

"Cade, if you're going to break up with me, just do it. I can take it. I'm not a child."

Cade shook his head. "I'm not breaking up with you ever, Jane. I plan to marry you."

"What?" Jane went from heartache to glee at his words. She threw herself into his arms, but Cade pulled back, staring down at her happy face.

"Jane, I need to tell you what was in my note. After you left that morning, your father called me. Bailey had disappeared again. Montgomery searched her computer and phone records and found out she had sneaked away to go back to Raul."

"Oh, God."

Cade put his arm around her shoulders. "He asked for my help, darlin', and since they were your family, I couldn't turn them down."

Jane's body tightened in fear at his words. "Were?"

"I caught a plane to Corpus Christi, but I was too late. Raul had already managed to get her across the border. Your dad flew down, determined to go inside and get her out again. I tried to warn him. I said I would go and went to get supplies, but when I came back, he was gone."

Jane started crying.

"Raul had contacted him while I was gone and told him, if he didn't give the money back, he would kill Bailey. He said he wouldn't transfer the money until he saw Bailey, so he went out to meet them without waiting for me to come back. It took me two weeks to find them. Their bodies are being flown back tomorrow. I'm sorry I couldn't save them for you."

Her father and sister were gone.

Numbness at his words quickly gave way to grief, and Cade held her as she cried, gently rocking her back and forth, whispering over and over how much he loved her. His words finally penetrated her sorrow.

"Bailey didn't want to be saved. She always believed that nothing bad could happen to her. Dad was the only one who could have made her change, but he wouldn't face what the true Bailey was like."

After a while and finally calming down, Jane stood up, taking his hand. "We're going to have dinner with our family and enjoy the rest of Christmas. Tomorrow, I'll make the arrangements…" Jane's voice broke.

They went back to the front room where everyone stopped eating as Jane and Cade took a seat at the table.

"Stud, can you pass the ham?" she asked politely, feeling like the food would choke her if she took a bite. She was trying to keep a brave face, not wanting to ruin their Christmas dinner with the sad news.

She filled her plate with all her favorites as Cade filled his.

"Skulls, can you pass the turkey?" Cade asked, reaching his hands out.

"Brother, you don't want the turkey. Try the ham." Skulls's wiggling eyebrows looked like a caterpillar moving across his brow.

"I prefer the turkey—"

"See, Skulls, not everyone likes ham for Christmas." A good-looking older woman dressed in a low cut glitter top that bared half her breasts stood up, hefting the untouched turkey closer to him. "Enjoy. I cooked it all by myself without any help from Sex Piston," she boasted.

"You're Sex Piston's mom?" At her nod, Cade turned to Jane. "Pass the ham."

Chapter Twenty-seven

Jane couldn't help the tears that fell down her cheeks as she watched her father's casket lowered into the ground. Then, minutes later, her sister's casket was also lowered.

Cade stood at her back, his arm around her waist, his warmth a buffer against the strong winds carrying flurries.

"Ready?" Cade asked.

"Yes." Jane turned away as the dirt was being shoveled onto their caskets.

They rode Cade's new motorcycle to the home of Sex Piston's parents, where Jane stood numbly as friends all offered their condolences.

She was surprised when her stepmother stepped hesitantly through the doorway. Jane took a step forward, hugging her usually standoffish stepmother. Her typically immaculately beautiful face was a mask of grief.

"I'm truly sorry, Delphi."

"Thank you, Jane. I wasn't sure I would be welcome, but I couldn't bear to be alone right now."

"I'm glad you came," Jane said sincerely. "Come on, let's get you something to eat."

Cade was amazed at Jane's loving concern for her stepmother. Before now, he was sure Delphi hadn't had the time of day for her stepdaughter.

Cade's eyes narrowed on Jane's mother, who moved away from the food-laden table when she saw who was with Jane, ugly jealousy marring her lined face.

Cade strolled casually across the room and came to a stop beside her. "Wipe that look from your face before Jane sees it. I'm not going to have her worrying about your shit today."

Jane's mother opened her mouth to reply.

"Shut it. I don't want to listen. Your days of having Jane jump are over. From now on, you're going to deal with me first. Your lazy ass is going to get a job, too. Popeye's is hiring, and the manager is expecting a call from you. Jane won't be funneling you any more money, which I'm sure you're counting on when her dad's house sells. Not going to happen. If there are any drugs in your house, you better get rid of them when you get home. Every day, I'm going to stop by, and if I find any of that shit in your house, I'm calling the cops. Unlike them, I don't give a fuck about search warrants."

"You can't—" she protested, nearly choking on her sandwich.

"Watch me. You're on probation. You get caught with drugs, and your ass will be back in jail and out of Jane's hair. That's a win-win for me. You're going to get clean whether you want to or not. You're going to piss in a cup for me once a week, and if it comes back positive, I'll call the cops. I'm going to be your worst fucking nightmare." Cade turned to leave the woman who was glaring a hole through him then turned back around. "Oh, and you better pray Jane's new car doesn't so much as get a scratch on it. Touch it, and I'll break every bone in that useless body of yours, and then I'll pick one of these big mountains surrounding us to bury you on."

Cade turned, nearly knocking down an eavesdropping Killyama.

"Let me know if you need any help after you do that bitch in. I'll dig the hole for you."

Cade's lips twitched. "I'd be afraid to go into those mountains with you alone after the way I treated Jane."

Killyama actually grinned at him. "You ain't in my sights, Cade. A week ago, I wouldn't have said that, but Fat Louise explained to us all that you had left a note. Any idea what happened to it?"

Cade searched her eyes, wondering if she was trying to see if he had lied to Jane. "No," Cade answered, lying as he watched Rock give Jane a cup of coffee. The fucking bastard was still chasing after his woman. He had no doubts who had taken his note.

"It's my fault, I should have called her and told her what was going on, I'm used to doing things on my own. It's a habit I intend to break."

"Ummhmm." Killyama's eyes followed his. "Still not happy with the way you treated my bitch at first, but she's forgiven you, and I don't want to see her hurt if I kill you, so that leaves me—"

"With giving me a friendly warning?"

"Seems to be the day for it, doesn't it?"

"Yeah, it does," Cade agreed before escaping the overpowering woman's presence.

Jane was still talking to Rock when he came to her side, taking the coffee cup out of her hands and ignoring Rock's angry glare. "Come on. There's something I want to show you." Taking her hand, he led her to the coat closet where he handed Jane her coat.

"I can't leave yet."

"We won't be gone long," Cade assured her, opening the door and then tugging her outside.

"Where are we going?" Jane asked as they walked down the driveway to the sidewalk.

Cade felt a lump in his throat at the trust she put in him.

"Right here." Cade led her up the walkway of a house next door to Sex Piston's parents.

"What are we doing here? No one lives here."

Cade took the key out of his pocket and opened the front door. "I do, or I will if you agree." He ushered her inside the empty house.

Her eyes widened at the inside of the home. "It's beautiful," she breathed.

"It's close to your friends and the clubhouse," Cade said softly, his voice filling the empty rooms. "I'm going to make an offer if you agree to move in here with me."

She turned to face him. "And if I don't?"

"Then I'll wait to buy a home until you are, but I can't guarantee the house will still be around. Of course, if you don't like this one, we can go together to find another. I just thought that—"

"Who told you?"

Cade smiled, cupping her cheek. "Sex Piston. She told me that, since you were teenagers, you planned to live in the same neighborhood. She doesn't exactly live next door anymore, but she comes by every day to check on her parents. I figured it would be close enough for you to still see her and your friends."

"You don't mind my friends?" Her amazed eyes stared up into his.

"Not so much. They take a little getting used to, but they're growing on me."

"Really?"

"Really." Cade's mouth brushed hers.

"Are you sure about buying the house? I mean, it will mean staying in one place, growing roots—"

"Growing roots isn't all I plan to do in this house. When you're ready, tell me and we'll get married and fill all the rooms upstairs with kids."

"That's a lot of commitment for you to take on." She leaned against him, letting him take all her weight.

"I'm looking forward to the challenge."

Jane reached into her pocket and pulled out her cell phone, handing it to him. "Call the realtor. I can't think of a better place."

With her standing in his arms, staring at him with love shining in her eyes, Cade thought she was the most beautiful thing he had ever seen. He didn't care about the four walls and a roof, all he needed was her.

Epilogue

"Allison, does this blanket come in blue?" Jane ran her fingertips over the soft pink baby blanket she had laid on the counter.

"It does, but I'm sold out of it. I can order it and have it here by the weekend."

"Okay, go ahead and order it. I'll pay for it and the other items." The counter was filled with baby goodies.

She had originally come to the Bag Boutique to wait for Sex Piston and the rest of the crew—they were going to have lunch at the Sizzler next door. When she hadn't seen their car outside, she had come inside with the intention to browse. To her surprise, Allison had designated a part of her designer store to merchandise for babies.

At first, Jane had leisurely strolled through the aisles, until a small giraffe caught her attention. From there, she had chosen several other items.

Allison began to ring up her purchases as Jane searched through her purse for her credit card. Her hand shook as she pulled her wallet out. She hadn't eaten much this morning, which was a no, no for her. She had intended to snack on a protein bar later that morning yet had become too busy at work. Her body was beginning to show the first warning sign that her sugar was running low. She needed to hurry and go next door for lunch.

"How's Stacy doing?"

Allison's mouth tightened at her question. "She's fine."

Jane blushed, belatedly realizing that her daughter would be a sore subject. Sex Piston had quit doing Allison's hair because Stacy had been caught bullying Meri and Sheri, Sex Piston's stepdaughters.

Jane tried her best to keep her gaze away from Allison's hair yet couldn't. It was very attractive, but it was the same style Jane had seen replicated on several women in town. The Cut Shop must only be able to cut hair in one style.

Jane brushed her own hair back from her cheek, beginning to perspire and feel even sicker. She wished Allison would finish.

The door opening behind her had both women turning.

"Hey, Rock, what are you doing in here?" Jane smiled. "Trying to buy a present for one of the women?" she teased.

"No." Rock didn't return her smile, his eyes on the counter. "I saw your car parked out front and thought I'd see if you wanted to grab some lunch."

"I'm already meeting Sex Piston and the rest of the crew. You're welcome to join us. Stud and Cade are also coming."

"I'll pass." His hand touched the pink baby blanket, his face going pale. "You're pregnant again?"

"No." Jane's expression lost her glow of happiness. "I'm buying this for Lily's baby."

"I thought Shade threatened everyone not to give her a

baby shower?"

"He did … but I thought…" Jane stumbled with her explanation at his expression. "Every baby needs a few new things. I know she has all Sex Piston's and Beth's babies hand me downs, but"—she reached out, touching the cute blue pacifier—"you can't reuse a paci"—her hand then touched a giraffe—"or a teether. These bottles are new, so the baby doesn't get as gassy."

"What are you doing, Jane?"

"What do you mean?" Her voice trembled at his harsh expression.

"You know what I see when I look at you?"

"No…" Jane turned back to the counter, sure she didn't want to hear what Rock was about to say.

She nodded to Allison for her to give the total.

"I see a woman desperately wanting what you can't have. You're buying Lily's baby all this overpriced shit for her baby instead of the one you lost. Just like you took Cade back knowing he's going to fuck around on you again. Your baby's gone, just like Cade will be. Accept it and move on."

"Who to? You?" Cade's voice came from the doorway as he strode inside, followed by her friends and Stud.

Rock didn't back down, though, and Jane's lips trembled. Rock had been her friend.

She started to reach out to touch his arm.

"Don't fucking feel sorry for him after what he just said to you."

Cade moved to stand between her and Rock. "I've had it with you chasing after my woman. I've put up with it because you were there for her when she needed someone, and I was too stupid—"

"Hell, you were fucking Demie the night she lost her kid."

Jane's face paled. She could tell from the haunted look on Cade's face that Rock was telling the truth.

Allison's eyes were wide as she listened. Her big mouth

would be spreading everything she was listening to all over town.

Cade lunged for Rock, nearly knocking him down. Rock managed to catch himself, though he did knock over a glass table with designer bags on it, shattering it. Rock's fist then swung out, smashing into Cade's face. Allison screamed as the shoving escalated into a bloody fight between the two bikers.

Rock tried to pin Cade against the counter, punching him in the stomach. Then Cade pushed Rock back with his shoulder, both of them taking down a rack of baby clothes.

"Stop it!" Jane yelled. She went to try to break them apart, but Sex Piston blocked her path.

"Don't you dare. I've got a hundred bucks on Cade beating him."

"Shit!" Crazy Bitch shouted at Rock. "Watch his left."

Sex Piston shrugged. "Crazy Bitch thinks Rock can whip his ass because Rock's bigger."

"He is, but Cade's meaner," Killyama gloated, giving away who she had betted on.

"They're going to get hurt!" Jane protested, still trying to move around Sex Piston.

Sex Piston shrugged. "They need to get it out of their system. Besides, Rock deserves it for taking Cade's letter, and Cade deserves to receive a few bruises for the way he treated you. I tried to get Stud to beat his ass for me, but he was determined to stay out of it. Said they'd go at it sooner or later. He's the one who gave me the idea for starting a betting pool."

"Who did Stud bet on?" Jane asked curiously, wincing as the two fighting men knocked down a whole shelf of stuffed animals.

Sex Piston grinned. "He told me he wouldn't bet against the brothers, but he said, if Cade won, he'd let me get my nipple pierced. If Rock wins, he'd get his cock pierced. I wouldn't mind losing a hundred bucks for that.

I'm tired of listening to Diamond bragging about Knox's." Sex Piston stared at Stud's crotch in his loose jeans. "I think he knew Rock was going to lose."

"You think?" Jane asked sarcastically. She couldn't imagine Stud letting anyone near his dick with a sharp object.

Cade finished the fight with a final kick to Rock's ribs as he lay on the floor, surrounded by a variety of stuffed animals and purses.

"Stay the fuck away from Jane. I'm not going to let her go, and I'm sure as shit not going to watch you try to steal her away from me."

Rock groaned as he tried to rise to his feet. Stud ended up stepping forward between the two men, reaching down to help Rock stand.

Rock started toward Cade again, but Stud held him back. "Cut it out, Rock. Go back to the club."

"I'm calling the cops," Allison threatened, picking up her cell phone.

"I'll pay for the damages," Cade spoke, wiping his bloody lip with a bib Jane had been about to purchase.

Jane jerked it away with a heated glare.

Sex Piston leaned casually against the counter. "Stop by the shop tomorrow, and I'll do your hair for free."

"That include highlights?" Allison asked.

"Yes."

Alison disconnected the call. "Okay, but he's still going to pay for all the damages." She nodded towards Cade.

Cade pulled out his wallet as he walked to the counter. "I'll pay for Jane's things, too."

"Jane?" Allison looked up from the register.

"He means me." Jane's voice wobbled. She needed to leave and go next door to the restaurant. She clutched at the counter, feeling lightheaded.

Cade opened his wallet, removing a tiny gel tube of glucose and handing it to her while he asked Allison to replace the bib he had wiped blood on.

Jane took the tube, surprised he carried it on him. Her friends all carried something on them. After all the years they had spent together, they were well aware of Jane's haphazard way of dealing with her hypoglycemia.

Allison ran the card then bagged Jane's purchases, handing her the bag.

"Thanks, Allison. I'm sorry for the mess." Jane didn't think Allison would reply, but a hard glare from Cade had her forcing an insincere smile.

Jane left the store and went into the restaurant next door, sliding into a large booth. Cade sat down next to her, and Jane set the bags down between them, creating a wedge.

Jane began to feel better from taking the gel when her friends and Stud piled into the booth. She studied the menu, avoiding Cade's eyes. When a tear fell onto the menu, she used her thumb to surreptitiously wipe it away.

By the time the waiter brought them glasses of water, the table was unnaturally quiet.

"Can I take your order?"

Jane glanced up when it was her turn to order. "I'm not hungry. Just bring me a glass of orange juice."

"Bitch, you need to—" Sex Piston began, only to be cut off by Cade.

"Bring us both the lunch special." Cade took her menu and his, handing them to the waiter.

"Don't let Rock upset you. He's pissed off because he heard you moved in with Cade," Stud explained.

"It wasn't cool of him to throw up Demie," T.A. snapped, and the women at the table nodded their agreement.

"If Cade hadn't done it, he wouldn't have been able to throw it up to my girl," Sex Piston snapped, glaring at Cade then at Jane. "Men are dumbfucks; they always cheat."

Stud's gaze darkened, and Jane saw the anger brewing between the couple.

"Stud didn't." Jane's statement had Cade's hand tightening on his glass of water.

"Only because he knew I would neuter him if he did."

"I didn't technically cheat. I wasn't in love with you then. Besides, you walked away from me, telling me it was only a one night stand." Cade quit trying to defend himself when the five women's expressions showed they clearly didn't agree with him.

"Even the score." Killyama leaned back in her seat so the waiter could set their platters of food down in front of them.

"How?" Jane asked, taking a bite of her rice.

"Find someone to fuck. Pay the bastard back," Killyama suggested.

"Who is she gonna fuck?" Crazy Bitch asked.

"She could fuck Rock," T.A. piped in.

Jane shook her head. "I don't want to hurt him."

As Cade's fork dropped to his plate, Jane had to hide her smile. He believed she was actually considering fucking another man as payback.

"She could fuck Rabbit," T.A. offered another sacrificial lamb.

"Hell no. The point is to make Cade jealous, not laugh his head off." Sex Piston shot that candidate down, but not without offering another victim. "How about Pike? Stud could order him to do it."

Stud shot his wife an incredulous look. "No, I can't."

"Not Pike; he's terrible at fucking," T.A. spoke without looking up from her plate.

"How do you know?" Crazy Bitch asked with a snicker. "You do him?"

"Once, and it wasn't any good. Bastard got off and left me hanging."

"Sounds like Train," Killyama muttered.

"That's it!" Crazy Bitch's hand slammed down on the table. "She can fuck one of The Last Riders."

"Not unless she wants to start a war."

While Cade was getting angrier by the second, Jane couldn't keep herself from provoking him further.

"Which one? Lucky?" Jane had always thought Lucky was the handsomest of The Last Riders.

"No!" Killyama looked like her refried beans were sour. "He's into that freaky-deaky shit. Rider would do you."

"She'd have to catch him first."

Stud winced when Sex Piston's pointed boot kicked him under the table.

"I like Rider," Jane pretended to consider the option. "He saved my life."

"No, he didn't. I did," Cade interrupted.

"You're also the one who cheated on me!" Jane yelled, letting her anger go. "You cheated on me the night I lost our baby!" She reached onto her plate before turning to Sex Piston. "Hold my Chimichanga." Jane picked her plate of food up and threw it at him.

"Let him have it." Killyama didn't stop eating to encourage her friend.

Cade couldn't dodge the plate of food in the tight confines of the booth. He scraped the food off and onto the table. "I thought we had settled this." Cade slid out of the booth. "I need to go to the bathroom and wash this off." He strode away without looking back at her.

"He's mad at me," Jane whispered, ashamed of her behavior.

"You think?" Sex Piston handed her the Chimichanga back before taking the check from the angry waiter who was going to have to clean up the mess when they left.

"I need to get back to work." Jane wanted to be out of there before Cade returned.

She took her bags and slid across the booth, trying to avoid the food. "I'll see you guys later."

Her friends all called out their goodbyes to her retreating back, and she had to blink back tears as she pushed the door open. Cade was so furious with her he might throw her out of their new house. She couldn't blame him, either. She had acted terrible. She should have waited until he came home before giving him hell about Rock's comment on Demie.

Jane ate her remaining lunch on the drive back to work, castigating herself for her behavior. Of all her friends, she was the most passive and laid back, letting herself forget that none of the other women had used grenades to blow anyone up ... as far as she knew. Well, maybe Killyama might have. She couldn't be sure. She would have to ask her.

Once Jane arrived back to work thirty minutes late, she admitted several patients for testing, the whole time thinking about Cade. She debated texting him several times to apologize yet couldn't bring herself to do it, still too hurt after finding out about Cade and Demie.

Jane clocked out at the end of the day, for once not anxious to go home. She sat in her office chair, tempted to go to Crazy Bitch's apartment to spend the night. Instead, she rose to her feet with a plan.

She sent a message to Sex Piston before starting her car. She knew exactly who she was going to fuck to pay Cade back.

* * *

Jane smoothed the white T-shirt down. Her tiny bra provided no barrier for her peaked nipples, and her leather pants were so tight they were about to cut off her circulation.

Opening the door to the clubhouse, she had to catch her balance in the impossibly high-heeled boots she was wearing. Jesus, she didn't know how Sex Piston made wearing the boots look so easy.

Her friends were already seated at a table with a bottle of tequila in front of them. Jane had no doubt they planned to entertain themselves by watching the show. They definitely could be a pain in the ass sometimes.

Jane spotted the brother she had every intention of seducing. She gave her breasts an extra bounce and made her hips sway as she walked across the floor. Provocatively, she leaned against the bar.

Demie, whose large breasts were stunningly displayed in her own white T-shirt, was working behind the bar. Jane refused to compare herself against the woman. Those days were over. From now on, she was determined to have more confidence in her own appeal.

"I'll take a beer, Demie." Jane silently dared the bitch not to wait on her.

Demie reached into the ice, handing her a beer while giving her a nasty look, before she retreated to the other side of the bar.

"Hi, I've seen you around the club the last couple of months, but I haven't introduced myself. I'm Fat Louise." She held her breath after introducing herself.

Cade paused at lifting his beer to his lips, turning to face her. He was silent a full minute before answering, "I'm Traveler."

"Cool name." She took a sip of her beer for courage. "Want to dance?"

"Yeah."

Fat Louise set her beer down on the counter then walked to the dance floor, avoiding her friends' snickers as they passed their table. "Call Me the Breeze" was playing as she began moving to the music, swaying in place and appreciating the way Traveler's hand went to her hips to bring her body closer to his. His thigh slid between hers, making her nipples tighten in arousal, at the same time his gaze dropped to her breasts.

"Hungry" played next. Jane shot Killyama, who was standing by the sound system, a reproachful look over Cade's shoulder.

They danced until the floor became too crowded, going back to the bar for their drinks.

"I want to be honest with you." Jane licked the drop of beer away that clung to her bottom lip. "I came here tonight to cheat on my boyfriend."

"Is that so?"

Fat Louise nodded her head. "I wanted to pay him back for cheating on me. You were going to be my revenge fuck."

"You change your mind?"

"Not exactly. I don't even know if he is my boyfriend anymore. I was mad and threw something at him today, so I'm pretty sure he's mad at me now." Fat Louise stared at the crowded dance floor, unable to meet his eyes.

"Speaking from a man's point of view, I'd say he was over it by now. Besides, I bet he was more mad that you left before he could talk to you."

"That's a failing of mine. I run away before I can be pushed away. The only time I'm brave is when I have my friends with me."

"That's not true. I heard what went down in Mexico. Seems to me, you took pretty good care of yourself then."

Fat Louise shook her head. "When I thought my sister had something I wanted, I ran instead of fighting for it. When Demie made a play for my man, I stood back and watched it happen. I ran like I always do and pretended I didn't want it, anyway. Do you think, if I had told him I cared about him, he wouldn't have cheated on me?"

Traveler stared her straight in the eyes. "Probably not. A man has his pride, though, especially if she mouths off in front of everyone that the night that changed his life was nothing but a one night stand to her."

"He was all over Demie before I made that comment," Fat Louise snapped.

"Maybe it was a lame assed attempt to make you jealous. It wasn't smart, and it sure as shit backfired on him. I know, if that happened to me, I would regret that I didn't play it smarter." Traveler shrugged. "I'm not one to give advice. I don't actually have a lot of experience with relationships. I've only been in love once in my life."

"For real?"

Traveler's lips twitched. "Yep, she's special. We just

moved in together, and I plan to marry her if she'll ever get around to making up her mind."

"It might take a long time," Fat Louise warned.

Traveler shrugged. "I have plenty of time, and she's worth the wait."

"She is?" Fat Louise's voice became choked with tears.

"Yes, she is."

"Even Sex Piston wasn't Stud's first love. He was married twice before her."

"You always compare men to Stud?" Traveler's shot her an angry glare.

"Women always use other men to pick out the characteristics they think are perfect so they'll know what to look for when choosing a man for themselves. Stud has a lot of good qualities: he's a good father, he's loyal, and he love's Sex Piston." Jane didn't try to keep her admiration of Stud out of her voice. Watching him and his relationship with his children had made her realize that not all fathers picked favorites.

"I'm not perfect, but I plan on being a great father. I will always remain loyal to my future wife, and I love Jane."

"I'm not perfect, either. And I love you, too." Jane's arm circled his neck, pulling his head down for a tender kiss.

Cade's arm went around her, tightening until she was crushed against him. His tongue parted her lips before he thrust it into her mouth, turning the kiss from tender to passionate in a heartbeat.

Jane tilted her head back, breaking the kiss. "I don't want to have revenge sex anymore." She had lost that desire when Cade had admitted she was his first love.

"How about make-up sex, then? I've heard that can be pretty good." Cade brought her mouth back to his as he lifted her off her feet, walking with her towards the back of the club-house.

Cade reached out to open the door, backing her into

the darkened bedroom. He closed the door behind him with a kick of his booted foot before flicking the light switch on.

Jane giggled. "Who's going to say sorry first?"

"I will." Cade took off his boots then unzipped his jeans, pulling them off.

"I'll go next." Jane had to sit down on the bed to pull off her boots. She then stood to shimmy the tight leather pants down her thighs.

Cade gave a low whistle of appreciation. "I like the way you apologize." Jane hadn't worn any underwear, and her cleanly shaved pussy gleamed in the soft light.

Cade tore off his T-shirt, stepping forward with a predatory grin. Jane wanted to play longer by teasing him with taking off her T-shirt slowly, but Cade wasn't in the mood for games any longer. His hand reached out, pushing her down to the bed before covering her with his body. Jane's excitement grew when his hands went to her thighs, parting them with a slight adjustment of his hips. A hard thrust had a strangled scream of pleasure tearing from her throat.

"Damn, I like the way you apologize." Jane's hand went to Cade's shoulders as he began to rhythmically fuck her.

"Give me time … I can do better."

Jane's whimpers filled the room as Cade proved true to his words. He used his mouth to push up her T-shirt then tugged her bra out of the way to find a nipple with his lips. His teeth grazed the tender bud, awakening a passion in her that demanded fulfillment.

Her lips went to his chest, exploring the firm flesh until she reached his nipple. Her tongue laved at the small nub, bringing a groan from Cade, inciting him to move faster within her.

Cade rose to his knees above her and continued to pound into her. Lifting her hips upward, he watched his cock slide in and out of her cunt.

He reached his hand out, taking one of her hands and placing it on her clit. "Feel how wet you are."

Jane felt Cade's control slipping as his gaze rested on her hand. She began to move her fingers over her clit while she thrust her hips upwards to meet his.

"I'm really sorry, Cade."

Cade's face was a tortured mask of frenzied need. Jane dropped her eyes, looking at him beneath her lowered lashes to see the slick glide of his cock sliding into her pussy.

"Baby, seeing this pussy is the only apology I need." Cade glided his thumb over the smooth flesh.

As Jane's back arched as she came on his cock, Cade shuddered, releasing his come into her clenching pussy. Jane trembled when Cade's arms went under her, lifting her until she was sitting up with his cock still inside of her. His hand went to her hair, using it to tilt her head back.

"I'm sorry I hurt you and wasn't there when you needed me. It will be the first and last time in our lives together that it happens."

Jane stared deep into his eyes, her arms circling his sides to hold onto the man she loved more than life. "Cade, if I could go back in time and change anything about our past, the only thing I would change is losing our baby." She gave him a sweet smile.

Cade had never imagined a time in his life when he would become choked up with emotion, but staring back at the sweet woman who was holding him as if she would never let him go nearly did him in.

"It doesn't bother you I'm not the perfect man of your dreams?"

Jane wiggled on his lap, feeling his cock hardening inside of her. "Cade, you'll always be the man of my dreams."

Books By Jamie Begley:

The Last Riders Series:

Razer's Ride

Viper's Run

Knox's Stand

Shade's Fall

Cash's Fight

Biker Bitches Series:

Sex Piston

Fat Louise

The VIP Room Series:

Teased

Tainted

King

Predators MC:

Riot

The Dark Souls Series:

Soul Of A Man

Soul Of A Woman

ABOUT THE AUTHOR

"I was born in a small town in Kentucky. My family began poor, but worked their way to owning a restaurant. My mother was one of the best cooks I have ever known, and she instilled in all her children the value of hard work, and education.

Taking after my mother, I've always love to cook, and became pretty good if I do say so myself. I love to experiment and my unfortunate family has suffered through many. They now have learned to steer clear of those dishes. I absolutely love the holidays and my family puts up with my zany decorations.

For now, my days are spent writing, writing, and writing. I have two children who both graduated this year from college. My daughter does my book covers, and my son just tries not to blush when someone asks him about my books.

Currently I am writing four series of books- The Last Riders, The Dark Souls, The VIP Room, and Biker Bitches series.

All my books are written for one purpose- the enjoyment others find in them, and the expectations of my fans that inspire me to give it my best. In the near future I hope to take a weekend break and visit Vegas that will hopefully be this summer. Right now I am typing away on my next story and looking forward to traveling this summer!"

Jamie loves receiving emails from her fans,
JamieBegley@ymail.com

Find Jamie here,
https://www.facebook.com/AuthorJamieBegley

Get the latest scoop at Jamie's official website,
JamieBegley.net

44509992R00133

Made in the USA
Lexington, KY
02 September 2015